JESUS THE SADGURU
AND
HIS DISCIPLESHIP

JESUS THE SADGURU
AND
HIS DISCIPLESHIP

Emmanuel Singh

Tercentenary Publication
2010

JESUS THE SADGURU AND HIS DISCIPLESHIP – Published by the Rev. Dr. Ashish Amos of Indian Society for Promoting Christian Knowledge (ISPCK), Post Box 1585, 1654 Madarsa Road, Kashmere Gate, Delhi-110006.

ISBN: 978-81-8465-094-5

Laser typeset by **ISPCK,** Post Box 1585,
1654 Madarsa Road, Kashmere Gate, Delhi-110006
Tel: 23866322, 23866323
e-mail: ashish@ispck.org.in   •ella@ispck.org.in
website: www.ispck.org.

Contents

Foreword

I am pleased to be given the opportunity to write the foreword for the book, *Jesus the Sadguru and His Discipleship.* Dr. Emmanuel Singh's book, which focuses on Jesus the *Sadguru*, was first published by Christashram Publication in 2004. It was formally released during the Yeshu Darbar Convention held in Lucknow on March, 5th, 2004. The book's success prompted us to use the book for training new followers of Christ in rural areas.

I congratulate Dr Emmanuel Singh on bringing out a revised edition of that book. This book, I believe, will surely help new disciples of "the sadguru" in standing up for Christ, who said, "If you wish to be My disciples, deny yourself, take up your Cross and follow Me."

I have read Dr. Singh's first book व्यवस्था बनाम मोक्ष. As this book is a work of great erudition and originality, I have requested Dr Singh to translate it into English, so that it could be used as a text book for our Christashram Discipleship Training Programme. I am happy to note that a revised edition of this book is due to be published this year.

Dr. Emmanuel Singh is a Bible scholar of undoubted erudition and a man of deep prayer. He is known for his electrifying lectures on biblical topics, especially discipleship of Christ in the Indian context.

I have nothing but praise for the efforts Dr. Singh has been making towards making Jesus known, loved and followed by our countrymen.

Rev. Fr. Leo. D'Souza
Swami Christanand Leo,
Lucknow

Preface

The book, *The Sadguru Jesus and His Discipleship,* has been revised to make it comprehensive and more understandable for readers who are seeking the ultimate goal of their lives through the age-old *Guru-Shishya* (Teacher-Taught) tradition. Every man or woman (except the fool) is a seeker after God or truth and ultimately longs for fellowship with his or her Creator. So this book is being presented to keep that longing burning. All Scriptures state that it is desirable for spiritual novices to seek their accredited teachers (gurus, rabbis, mullahs, etc.) for their enlightenment and for reaching the goal of their lives.

In the Bible, we find that the invisible God sent the *Sadguru* (True-Teacher) into the world. He was recognised and accepted by His disciples as the visible form of the invisible God (John 3:2; 13:13; Col 1; 15; Heb 1:1-3).

I hope, readers will go through the book and search in Jesus Christ the marks and attributes of the *Sadguru* and verify the claims of Jesus the *Sadguru* when He says, "I am the Way, the Truth and Life. No one comes to the Father (God) except through Me" (Jn 14:16). "You search the scriptures because you think that in them you have eternal life; and it is they that bear witness to Me; yet you refuse to come to Me that you may have life" (Jn 5:39-40).

I must thank Acharya R.S. Verma, who invited me to Sattal (Nainital), in 2003, to speak on this topic, for which I got a great guideline from our very senior and learned teacher, Acharya D.P. Titus. Also, I am very grateful to Acharya Christanand Leo (the Publisher, Christashram, Lucknow), for encouraging and enabling me to write a book on this subject, which he published in 2004 (the first edition).

I am sure, the true seekers of truth will see the true light and marks of the *Sadguru* in Lord Jesus Christ (Jn 1:9) and reflect the same by being the light and salt of the earth (Matt 5: 13-14).

Emmanuel Singh

Allahabad

Part 1
Jesus the Sadguru

CHAPTER 1

Importance of the Guru

Gurus are teachers. They are of two types:

- Shiksha Guru (शिक्षा गुरू), *who imparts only secular truths, worldly knowledge* (apara vidya, अपरा विद्या) *and*
- Deeksha Guru (दीक्षा गुरु), *who imparts transcendental or divine truths* (para vidya, परा विद्या)

The Guru is a spiritual master (*gu* means darkness; *ru* means light). So, the one who dispels the darkness of ignorance (*avidya*, अविद्या) is called Guru.The Guru dispelling the spiritual darkness (darkness of ignorance and darkness of soul) is the Supreme need of mankind.

In our culture, Gurus were adored. There has been a wonderful *Guru-Shishya* (Teacher-Taught) relationship along with *Guru-Bhakti* (adoration of a teacher). In Sant-literature, the role of Guru has specific recognition. Sant Kabir says, there is none in the world like *Sadguru* (true teacher) who can lead to spirituality. Guru is the greatest well-wisher. Guru has the wonderful spiritual power to transform a disciple, from man to divine; therefore, it is natural for the seekers to be grateful to him for such an act of kindness.

The Guru is indispensable in both Hinduism and Christianity, as it is the Guru who directs the journey to *moksha* (liberation or redemption). It is the Guru who teaches and imparts spiritual or divine knowledge and directs divine ways to the aspirants or seekers who come to him. In Hindu tradition, a Guru is almost indispensable to progress in spiritual pilgrimage to union with God. The touch of the Guru can remove all evil tendencies of the aspirant (seeker). When the disciple is ready, the Guru appears, they say (Christ's promise of His presence in Matthew 18:20; James 4:8).

It is only the Guru who can teach the scriptures with authority and it is he who grants sacrament (*deeksha samskara*, दीक्षा संस्कार), a symbolic religious ceremony, especially baptism (baptism meaning to dip and wash in water, जल संस्कार or स्नान संस्कार, or ज्ञान स्नान [*jnana-snanam*] as translated in Tamil Bible), *eucharist* (भोज संस्कार or परम प्रसाद), etc.

Kabir Amrit Vaani (कबीर अमृत वाणी) expresses the importance of the Guru in the following manner:

> Guru bin kaise laag paar (This means, how can I reach the shore without a Guru?)

> Guru is One who can be reached for true guidance and Shishya (disciple) is one who is ready to learn. Without accepting these two well-defined roles, no relationship of Guru-Shishya (Teacher-Taught) can be established.

> Real knowledge does not emerge without the contact of a Guru. Salvation cannot be available without (the guidance of) the Guru. No one can get the glimpse of Truth without the Guru (showing the path) and none can get rid of his vices without (the help) the Guru.

> As soon as the brightness of knowledge lights up your heart, be sure that Guru has come to you because he breaks up the gloom of ignorance and you reach your Exclusive Identity.

As soon as one feels that all worldly attachments, happiness and sorrows are fading away, he should know that the Guru has come to him.

The disciple is filled with dirt from so many births, but the Guru is the water of knowledge purifying the disciple in minutes.

You may get everything by getting a Guru. If not, you have actually nothing. Every ordinary person has got a father, son or brother at his home but Guru is rare to be found.

Guru Gita (*Vishwasar tantra*) holds Guru like this:

Salutations to the Guru, who introduced to me the ultimate Reality that pervades the whole conscious or unconscious universe.

Salutations to the Guru who opens up the eyes of the disciple blinded by the darkness of ignorance through application of medicinal stick of knowledge.

For centuries preceptors have been the torch-bearers of an ancient tradition that has emphasised on imparting knowledge and wisdom in order to enhance the spiritual wealth of devotees. So, it is desirable for a spiritual novice to seek a Guru who may have the power to transform his whole personality (when the novice is ready, the Guru appears). The Guru must be served with implicit faith and complete obedience.

A true teacher is called *Sadguru;* all seekers of truth need him. A popular Christian hymn writer has rightly said, "I need Thee every hour I need Thee, O'my Saviour...."

CHAPTER 2

Views about the Guru

There are different views about the guru. Let us take a look at some of them.

(i) Traditional Salutations Collected as Guru Vandana or Guru-Gita: Guru–Vandana

Guru, the preceptor, is called 'Aadi,' i.e., the originator of all knowledge. He can also be called 'Anaadi,' i.e., without any starting point, because he is omnipresent. The Guru is the ultimate Godhead. There is nothing better or beyond the Guru.

"Guru is One, i.e., All in All in his field, omnipresent, purity personified, unchangeable by outside forces, unbiased evaluator of everyone's intelligence, unfathomable even by thoughts, un-influenced by any of the three *Gunas–Sattva* (the righteous virtue), *Rajas* (the passion in human beings) or *Tamas* (the evil nature). My salutations are offered to that Guru who is a storehouse of all virtues."

"Guru is consciousness, eternal, undisturbed, his presence is not limited even by the sky, unblemished, and beyond all starting points or *Naad* or any form of art. Salutations to that Guru is being offered."

"Guru is Brahma, the creator (of spiritual awareness/ initiating spiritual awakening), Guru is Vishnu, the nourisher (promoting the spiritual thoughts and activities), Guru is Maheshwar, the Destroyer (all of ignorance). Guru is actually Parabrahma, the Supreme reality. Salutations to the Guru!"

"Even if I transform all the earth as paper and all the vegetation as pens with all the oceans as ink, I shall not be able to write out the qualities of the Guru." (Sant Kabir Das).

(ii) Guru is a Stream and a Channel of Knowledge

Swami Rama (a swami living with Himalayan Masters) says, "After the mother has given birth to a child, and the parents have raised the child, the role of the guru begins, and he helps him fulfill the purpose of his life. A guru is different from a teacher. In India, this word is used with reverence and is always associated with holiness and the highest wisdom. It is a very sacred word. Guru is called Gurudev (an enlightened master), a holy man of God.

"There is a vast difference between an ordinary teacher, शिक्षा गुरु (imparting secular worldly knowledge, *apara vidya*) and a spiritual master, दीक्षा गुरु (imparting transcendental or divine truths, *para vidya*). The guru gives a saving word to his disciple. That is called mantra initiation. He (the spiritual master) removes obstacles, teaches his disciples how to make decision, remain peaceful and tranquil. He says to his student to make his mind one-pointed. He does so much for his student, and in return, wants nothing. Such people are called gurus. They guide humanity. As the sun shines and lives far above, the guru gives his spiritual love and remains unattached. The guru is not a physical being. Those who think of the guru as a body or a man do not understand this pious word. If a guru comes to think that his power is his own, then he is a guide no more. The guru is tradition; he is a stream of knowledge. That stream of knowledge goes through many channels.

"No human being can ever become a guru. But when a human being allows himself to be used as a channel for receiving and transmitting by the power of powers, then it happens. And for that, a human being should learn to be selfless. Genuine gurus cannot live without selflessness, for selfless love is the very basis of their enlightenment. They radiate life and light from the unknown corners of the world. The world does not know them, and they do not want recognition.

"Guru is not the goal. Guru is like a boat for crossing the river. It is very important to have a good boat, as it is very dangerous to have a boat that is leaking. But after you have crossed the river, you don't need to hang on to your boat, and you certainly don't worship the boat. Many fanatics think they should worship a guru. A guru should receive your love and respect that is different from worship. If my guru and the Lord come together, I will go to my guru first and say, 'Thank you very much, you have introduced me to the Lord.'"

(iii) *Shruti* (श्रुति) in Chandogya Upanishad (4.4.3 and 4.14.1)

The Guru is above the Vedas, since the knowledge given by him alone can lead to liberation from bondage.

(iv) Advaitarak Upanishad, 16, says that guru is the dispeller of the darkness of the soul.

(v) Shri Mahabharat (Vana-Parva 313.117) says: "Logic is not stable; Vedic scriptures differ; there is no Sage whose opinion is proof-worthy. The truth of *dharma* lies hidden in unseen caves. The way to *moksha* is that which a great soul or Guru has trodden" (Vana-Parva 313. 117, and also quoted by Acharya Daya Prakash in fulfillment of the Vedic Quest in Lord Jesus Christ, p 78).

(vi) "Guru is God-manifest, (सगुण ब्रह्म), none alse" (Shruti Brahm Vidya Upanishad 31)

(vii) "Guru to be Param Brahman, परमब्रह्म, Supreme God"(Advaitarak Upanishad, 17)

(viii) "The Guru is none other than *Saccidananda*" (the triune God of Vedanta philosophy)

(ix) The Bible recognises only one person as the guru or teacher "Nor are you to be called `teacher' for you have one teacher, the Christ" (Mathew 23: 10).

(x) Sat-tal Christian Ashram (Nainital) holds: "CHRIST IS THE GURU OF THIS ASHRAM." Christians perform Guru-Bhakti (Supreme devotion) to God alone who is revealed in the Guru, the Lord Jesus Christ. The Apostles of Jesus never accepted any *guru-bhakti* offered to them by people.

(xi) According to the writers of the Granth, more clearly still the invisible God reveals Himself to the devout soul in the personality of the holy teacher, the Guru. For the Sikh the Guru is what a Divine incarnation is to the Hindu. In phrases that agree almost word for word with the Gospel of John, the Granth proclaims that the Guru is the *Deus visibilis* ("God Himself in Person"): "The Guru is God and God is the Guru; there is no difference between them. God and the Guru are one. The Word is the Guru, the Guru is the Word. The Guru is the Creator, the Guru is the Artist; without the Guru there is nothing; what the Guru wills, that happens. O God, the Guru has shown Thee to mine eyes."

As incarnate God the Guru appears as the only mediator, the way to *Parameshwar* (the "Lord of All"):

> Without the Guru man has no love for God, the filth of selfishness cannot be removed."
>
> (Nanak)

> The true Guru is the true Lord, through His Word Union with God is achieved."
>
> (Amar Das)

> Without the true Guru no man can reach perfection. The Guru is the guide, the Guru is the boat, the Guru is the raft...the Guru is the *tirth* (the sacred tank) and the ocean."
>
> (Nanak)

> Nanak even says, 'A man hath come by whose favour the whole world shall be saved.'
>
> (*The Gospel of Sadhu Sundar Singh* by F. Heiler, p 26)

CHAPTER 3

Qualities of the Guru

According to the Upanishads and other Hindu scriptures, the Guru is one who is:

(i)   God (and therefore not in bondage); (Brahma Vidya Up., 31).

(ii)   Learned in Scriptures (Shrotiyam-Mundak Up., 1.2.12).

(iii) Established in God (Brahma Nishtham Mundak Up., 1.2.12)

(iv)   Brahmachari (celibate) (Atharva Veda, 11.5.17)

(v)   Chaste in character (Panini, 4.4.98)

(vi)   Nirmal (pure)

(vii) Free from dualities (*Nirdvanda*)

(viii) All-knowing (omniscient)

(ix)   Unattached to lust (Anasakta) (Kularnava Tantra, 13.38-50)

(x)   Saviour and refuge (Vivek Chudamani, 34-36)

In addition, our saints have told us how to choose and identify the proper guru by giving heed to their proper words:

The ideal disciple would surrender his all;
The ideal Guru accepts nothing at all.

If the Guru is blind (without eyes of spiritual wisdom), the disciple is bound to be totally blind (without the eyes of spiritual knowledge). If a blind person gets another blind to guide him, who is going to show the true path?

Gurus hold differing thoughts and ideas. He is to be revered whose words reveal the real technique for knowing God.

The Guru being covetous, his disciple is greedy;
Both will stumble together in hell.
The Guru should be like knife-sharpner,
Which removes all rust within a moment.

A Guru must be correctly recognised before acceptance. People can be deceived by false teachers, false Christs or false prophets. Jesus warns His disciples and followers:

Take heed that no one leads you astray. For many will come in My name, saying, 'I am the Christ,' and they will lead many astray (Matt 24:4, 5).

For false Christs and false prophets will arise and show great signs and wonders, so as to lead astray, if possible, even the elect. Lo! I have told you before hand. So if they say to you, 'Lo! He (Lord Jesus Christ) is in the wilderness,' do not go out; 'Lo! He is in the inner rooms,' do not believe it (Matt 24:24-26).

By being careful about selecting a guru, one can differentiate between the Sadguru (true-teacher) and a number of so-called gurus or *bhagwans* who make their appearance in both Hinduism and in Christianity. Most of these god-men live in luxury and lead a self-centred life. They are like leaking boats and blind guides.

The learned Vedic sages were also aware of the fact that a real Sadguru was hard to find (Kularnava Tantra 13.99.13; Vivek Chudamani 3).

Let us consider what the Bible and Guru Nanak have to say regarding false teachers.

False Teachers
"The spirit (the spirit of truth/the spirit of God) clearly says that in the later times some will abandon the faith and follow deceiving spirits and things taught by demons. Such teaching came through hypocritical liars, whose consciences have been seared as with a hot iron. They forbid people to marry and order them to abstain from certain foods which God created to be received with thanks giving by those who believe and who know the truth" (1 Tim 4:1-3).

False Believers
"For the time will come when men will not endure sound doctrine. Instead, to suit their own desires, they will gather around a great number of teachers to say what their itching ears want to hear. They will turn their ears away from the truth and turn aside to myths (2 Tim 4:3-4).

Danger of False Teachers
"But there were false prophets among the people, just as there will be false teachers (Gurus) among you. They will certainly introduce destructive heresies, even denying the Sovereign Lord who bought them–bringing swift destruction on themselves. Many will follow their shameful ways and will bring the way of truth into disrepute. In their greed these teachers will exploit you with stories they have made up. Their condemnation has long been hanging over them, and their destruction has not been sleeping" (2 Pet 2:1-3).

Nanak Warns Against Mendicant Friars

"Do not revere those who call themselves *guru* and *pir* (an Arabic expression for a guru) and who beg for alms. Only those who live by the fruits of their labour and do honest and useful work in the way of truth. Ye should live as hermits in your own homes."

Nanak further disapproves of the rigid asceticism of the *brahmans*, *yogis* and *sanyasis*: "To burn a limb in the fire, to stand in water, to fast, to endure great heat and cold, to hold one arm up for a long time together, to stand upon one leg — all these works of penance are works of darkness."

CHAPTER 4

Jesus Christ Fulfills the Role of the Sadguru

When we look to the historical figure of Jesus Christ, we discover in Him the marks of the Sadguru.The aspirations, speculations and philosophy of seekers find embodiment (fulfilment) of the religious truth in the life of Lord Jesus Christ. (John 3:2)

In his book, *The Idealist View of Life*, Dr. S. Radhakrishnan, the great philosopher of our land, observed 'religious truth' in the following manner: "The Religious Truth is found in Plato and Upanishads. Its embodiment is in the life of Jesus."

Now let us consider the character of Lord Jesus Christ fulfilling the role of the Sadguru in the light of the scriptures mentioned below:

(i) Upanishads and other Hindu Scriptures

Being full incarnation of God, Jesus is without bondage. He is *nirmal* (pure and holy), sinless, omniscient (all-knowing), saviour (*trata*) and refuge, *brahmachari* (follower of God and celibate), *sanyasi* or *vairagi* (having no self-desire, pride or passion), *karmayogi* (who did nothing for his own reward, but was the fountain of love and *ahimsa*), all powerful (to heal, forgive and save sinners by His own vicarious suffering, making the believer eligible for Eternal life), whose followers would never stumble and would ever walk in the light. So, Jesus fulfils the Vedic quest for the fulfilment of the role of the Sadguru.

(ii) **The Bible**

Jesus is the Sadguru (true-teacher) because He is the light of the world as God is (1 Jn 1:5; Jn 8:12; 9: 5; Jn 1 : 9); He can therefore dispel the darkness of ignorance or of soul. We may not know the future but we have to move on, unaware of the consequences of our actions. Only the light of our True-Teacher (Guru) can be the lamp unto our feet and light unto our path. The teachings of our Sadguru never allow us to stumble.

Jesus is the One who came to redeem humanity from sin by bearing the punishment of our sin (Jn 1:29; 1 Pet 1: 18-19; 1 Cor 6:20; Matt 1:21, etc.).

Jesus is God, both manifest and un-manifest (Col 1:15; Jn 1:1, 3, 14; Deut 18: 15-19; Phil 2:5-8; Col 2:9, etc.).

Jesus is full and final incarnation of God (Heb 1:1-4; Col 2:9; Jn 1:14, 18)

Gurutva of Jesus Christ can be further affirmed as follows:

(1) **Jesus is Blameless, Holy and Sinless**

He was born of Virgin Mary by the creative power of the Holy Spirit (Mt. 1:18-25; Lk. 2:1-5; Isaiah 7:14).

Four major religions of the world bear witness to the sinlessness of Jesus Christ. They are (1) Hebrew Scriptures called the Old Testament (Isaiah 53; 9; 7:14); (2) Islam; in *i Sura Maryam* of the Quran Sharif, the sinlessness of Jesus and Mary, the Virgin Mother, is declared; (3) In the *Bhavishya*

Purana of the Hindus, an Indian king, while visiting Palestine and on enquiring the name of a sage whom he met and who was fair complexioned and white clothed, got the answer that he was known as Jesus Christ, mighty king, blameless person, Son of God, born of Virgin. The Sage counselled king (Shalivahan) that God should be worshipped in righteousness, truth and pure openness of mind (*Bhavishya Puran*, Khand III, P 231); (4) *The Gospels* (Matt 1:18-25; Luke 2:8-15)—the angel's message to Virgin Mary and the Shepherds about the virgin, sinless birth of Jesus Christ. Jesus himself challenged His accusers saying, "which of you convicts Me of sin?" (John 8:46)

(2) **Jesus Christ—the Eternal Word of God, Creator and Pre-existent**
Both the Bible and the Vedanta speak of God as the 'Word', the *shabda*, who is the creative principle of the universe.

The Gospel of John 1:1, 3 speak of Christ: "In the beginning was the word, and the Word was with God, and the Word was God. Through Him all things were made; without him nothing was made that has been made" (Jn 1:1, 3 Cf. Col 1:16-17). The unseen God became manifest (visible) to the world through Christ, His Word. (Jn 1:14; Deut 18:15-19; Jn 17:5).

> The Word is Brahma [God] (Br. Ar. Upanishad 1.3.21; 4.1.2 and Brahmvindu Upanishad 17).

> The Word is *Akshara* (imperishable) and *Pra-Brahma* (the Absolute God)–(Brahmvindu Up 16)

> The Word (of Rgveda 10.125) is the creative Principle of the universe.

(3) **Jesus—Sadguru from God (John 3:2)**
Nicodemus, a member of the Jewish ruling council, came to Jesus at night and said, "Rabbi (my teacher) we know

you are a teacher who has come from God. For no one could perform the miraculous signs you are doing if God were not with him."

Jesus' disciples and others used the title 'Guru' for Jesus at various occasions (Mt 23:7-8; Jn 1:38, 49; 3:2, 26; Jn 1:38; 6:25; 20:16). The term *Rabbi* literally means 'Teacher.' Jesus accepted Himself as Sadguru (Jn 13:13, 16; Lk 6:40; Jn 15:20 (Cf Lk 22:27; Mt 10:24).

(4) **St. Peter declared Jesus as God's Messiah (Mt 16:13-19; Mk 8: 27-29)**

(5) **An angel proclaimed the virgin birth of Jesus the Sadguru (Mt 1:18-25)**

(6) **An angel proclaimed the birth of Jesus the Sadguru to the Shepherds (Lk 2:8 - 20)**

(7) **Jesus was sent by God**

Jesus said: "For I have come down from heaven, not to do My own will, but the will of Him (God the Father) *who sent Me.* No one can come to Me unless the *Father who sent Me* draws him; and I will raise him up at that day. ...And *He who sent Me is with Me.* The Father has not left Me alone, for I always do those things that please him." (Jn 6:38, 44; 8:28-29)

(8) **The Purpose of Jesus' coming**

Jesus said, "The Spirit of the Lord is upon Me, Because He has anointed Me to preach the gospel to the poor. He has sent Me to heal the broken hearted, to preach deliverance to the captives And recovery of sight to the blind, To set at liberty those who are oppressed, To preach the acceptable year of the Lord" (Isa 61:1-2; Lk 4:18-19).

(9) Jesus has Extraordinary Wisdom

His extraordinary wisdom was exposed when He was 12 years old. He had astonished the learned religious leaders (Scribes and Pharisees) of His time in the temple of Jerusalem (Lk 2:46-47). The activities of His life between the age of 12 and 30 are not clearly known; may be, He was preparing Himself for mystical truths, inseparable union and communion with God the Father for his earthly public ministry, which commenced when He was 30 years old.

(10) Jesus the Sadguru is our Creator (Gen. 1:26; Eph 2:10; Col 1:15-17).

Then God said, 'Let us make man in our image' (Gen 1:26).

For we are God's workmanship, *created in Christ Jesus* to do good work, which God prepared in advance for us to do (Eph 2:10).

He is the image of the invisible God, the first born over all creation. For by Him all things were created: things in heaven and on earth, visible and invisible, whether thrones or powers or rulers or authorities; *all things were created by Him and for Him.* He is before all things, and in Him all things hold together (Col 1:15-17).

(11) Jesus the Sadguru has amazing healing powers (Mt 9: 18-26; Mk 5:21-43, etc.)

(12) The transfiguration of Jesus during prayer on a high mountain

During transfiguration His (Jesus') face shone like the sun, and His clothes became as white as the light. Just then there appeared before them Moses and Elijah, talking with Jesus ... soon a bright cloud enveloped them, and a voice from the cloud said (for Jesus), "This is My Son, whom I love; with Him I am well pleased. Listen to Him." When the disciples heard this, they fell face down to the ground, terrified. But Jesus came and touched them when they looked up, they saw no one except Jesus. (Mt 17: 1-8; Mk 9:2-8).

(13) Jesus answers the question 'Who is the Greatest?'
"...Jesus sat down, called the twelve disciples, and said to them, "If anyone desires to be first, he shall be last of all and servant of all." Then He took a little child and set him in the midst of them. And when he had taken him in His arms, He said to them, "Whoever receives one of these little children in My name receives Me; and whoever receives Me, receives not Me but Him who sent Me." (See Matt 18:1-5; Mk 9:33-37; Lk 9:46-50)

(14) Jesus offers Rest to the Weary (See Mt 11:25-30; 13:16-17)

(15) Jesus is the source of prayer (See Mt 6:5 , 9-13; 7:7-11; Lk 11:9-13; Heb 5:7-10; Mt 26:36-46, etc).

(16) Jesus' Teaching About true Happiness
"... a woman spoke up from the crowd and said to Him, 'How Happy (blessed) is the woman who bore you and nursed you!' But Jesus answered, 'Rather, how happy are those who hear the word of God and obey it!'" (Luke 11:27-28)

(17) The Disciples are Mother and Brothers of the Sadguru
Pointing to His disciples Jesus said to the crowd, "Here are my mother and brothers. For whoever does the will of My Father in heaven is my brother and sister and mother" (See Mt 12: 49-50; Mk 3:31-35; Lk 8:19-21).

(18) Jesus—the deliverer of the world—was prophesied long before His birth (See Isa 9:2; 61:1-2; Lk 4:18-19)

(19) Jesus—the wisdom and power of God

Paul says that Christ has become for us the wisdom from God, that is, our righteousness, holiness and redemption. (See 1 Cor 1:30; 2:9-10; Mt 22:29; Jn 17:3; Hosea 4:6; Pr. 4:7; 2 Pet 3:18)

(20) Jesus— the Omniscient God

"He knows all that is knowledgeable; no one knows him" (Shvet. Up. 3.19)

Jesus Christ, the Word of God, had complete knowledge of all things, in the oneness of the Godhead. He was the visible image of the invisible God (Col 1:15). He is everlasting Father (Is 9:6). Jesus has always been as God is. But he did not consider equality with God—something to be grasped (Phil 2:6). Jesus said, "My Father and I are one" (Jn 10:30); He said to one of his disciples, "For a long time I have been with you all and yet you do not know Me?" (Jn 14:9). God suffered in Christ on the Cross (Acts 20:28). He did not need men's testimony about man, for He knew what was in a man (Jn 2:24-25). Sitting at the well, Jesus knew all the inner life of the Samaritan woman who had come to draw water (Jn 4:18-19). Nathanael (one of His disciples) was seen of Him under a fig tree even before Nathanael came into His presence (Jn 1:48-50).

Jesus knew that He was sent into this world by God the Father (Jn 4:34; 5:37); He knew which fish had a coin in its mouth, with which the temple tax could be paid; He knew which disciple would betray him; He knew that He would suffer and die for the sins of mankind, and also rise up again from the dead; He knew that He would come again at the end of the age; He knew that He had all authority in heaven and on earth (Matt 28:18); He knew the glory He had with the Father before the world was made (Jn 17:5).

Some of the great sayings (महावाक्य) of Jesus in John's Gospel are well known. Jesus says: "Without Me you can do nothing" (Jn 15:5); "I and Father are one" (Jn 10:30); "No one has seen the Father except the Son" (Jn 1:18); "I come from the Father and return to the Father" (Jn 13:3; 16:28); "My words are spirit and life" (Jn 6:63); "I am the Way, the Truth, and the Life"(Jn 14:6:15:5); "I am the Bread of life"(Jn 6:35,41); "I am the light of the world" (Jn 1:9:8:12); "I am the Resurrection and the Life" (Jn 11:25); "I am the Good shepherd" (Jn 10:11, 14); "I am the door" (Jn 10:9; 14:6); "He who has seen Me has seen the Father" (Jn 14:9); "No one comes to the Father, except through Me" (Jn 14:6).

Jesus was the visible image (manifest God, *Saguna Brahma*) of the invisible God (Un-manifest God, *Nirguna Brahma*). Ramanuj acharya, Brahma Sutra, Dr. S. Radhakrishnan, Acharya Vinoba Bhave and others identify the manifest God with the absolute (*nirguna* or un-manifest God), that is, the absolute is both the Un-manifest and the Manifest.

The Bible says that God is one, expressed in the triune form of the Father, the Son and the Holy Spirit, *which are one is essence* in the unity of the Godhead; their expressions may be particular. The three-in-one share the attributes of one another, in the area of love, righteousness, justice, creation, knowledge, etc.

Creation is attributed to the Father, to the Son and to the Holy Spirit (Gen 1:26). The Father loves the world as much as does the Son. The Father suffered at the Cross in the Son (Acts 20:28). In the same manner, the 'knower,' in the Upanishads is the eternal *shabda* (word).This eternal word is Christ (un-manifest becoming manifest).

(Fulfilment of the Vedic Quest in the Lord Jesus Christ by Acharya Daya Prakash)

The omniscient Jesus knows everything. He knows you and me; He knows our predicament and its best treatment as well. The Eternal Word of God, Jesus, the Sadguru (the light of the world), knows us as we are. We hardly know ourselves. Only 10 per cent of our life-area is exposed; the rest of our worldly-laden and worldly-yoked life is unknown to us. This heavy-laden life needs a burden-mover and burden-lifter to expose the full life-area of man for enjoying an abundant full life (Jn 10:10). Jesus is really the most needed Sadguru (Jn 13:13). So, Jesus gives great invitation to all the weary and heavy-laden people of all nations, race, creed, culture, etc., to come to Him to receive rest in Him by being united or yoked to Him and to learn how to live in this world and how to escape from drowning in an ocean of sin and how to swim safely with Him (Matt 11:28-30).

People of this *kaliyuga* or difficult times of this last or end age should not turn a deaf ear to the great loving, saving, peaceful and restful invitation of our all-knowing God, Jesus Christ, who knows well how the ungodly people of this earth will face the coming great tribulation and their self-invited destruction in the world in the near future (Matthew 24; Mark 13; Luke 21; 2 Peter 3; Revelation chapters 12-18; Daniel 12; Ezekiel 38 and 39; Zechariah 12 and 14; Joel 3:1-16, etc.) And He also knows well how the righteous (*dharmatma*) people of this earth will have the full hope and confidence to live in a new heaven and a new earth (See Revelation chapters 21 and 22) and would live to have an everlasting blissful life with their Creator (2 Pet 3:13; Matt 13:43, Matt 8:11).

(21) Christ–a great *Sanyasi* or *Vairagi*

Sanyasi means "renunciation of world (cf Jn 17:16)." Jesus had no self-desire, pride or passion (Cf. Maitriya Up. 2. 17-18). He was a great *vairagi*, as He had nothing of his own. Jesus said, "Foxes have holes, birds of the sky have nests, the Son of Man has no place to put His head" (Luke 9:58).

Sanyas and *vairag* have been known and practised in Christianity, especially during the Middle Ages in Europe. St. Thomas, one of the disciples of Jesus, who came to India (in 46A.D.), Sadhu Sundar Singh and Kartar Singh (Sikh sadhus of Punjab) and some Garhwali sadhus were all *sanyasi* and *vairagi* known to the Christian world.

(22) Jesus–the *Karmayogi*

Like a *karmayogi* (desireless of fruit or reward), Jesus went about doing good and healing all who were oppressed by demons or devils. He forgave the sinner, raised the dead and fed the multitude, but not for his own reward. Having no fear of being defiled, he would go near the leper, the blind and the dead to touch and heal them. Jesus gave a new dimension to holiness.

(23) Jesus the Saviour

The Vedas have recognised sin as the bond (बन्धन) (अविद्या or ignorance) that prevents the person in bondage from attaining union with the Lord. The sinner is likened to a calf chained to a post (Rgveda 2.28.5-6; Yajur Veda 8.13). It is transgression against the law (*dharma*) of God (Rgveda 7.89.5), or something done against brother, friend, neighbour or stranger (Rgveda 5.85.7-8).

According to the Bible, sin is transgression or breaking of God's commandments (1 Jn 3:4); It is man's rebellion and disobedience against his Maker (Deut 9:7; Joshua 1:18).

The bondage is the lost condition of man who has wandered away from home.

Lord Jesus Christ illustrated this 'lost' character of the sinner through terms such as 'the lost sheep,' 'the lost coin' or 'the lost son' (Luke 15; Cf. Chh. Up. 6.14.1-2).

This sin is universal, "All have sinned and fallen short of the glory of God" (Rom 3:23) and no one is righteous before God (Psalm 143:2) Bhagavad-Gita (18.40) says that none is free from the threefold (passion, anger and greed) binding nature, which is known as *triguna*.

Sin is in the very nature of man and its seed exists in our nature (Ps 51:5; Rom 5:12, 19). It is impossible to cure the sinful nature of man by human effort alone. The Bible tells us that a black man cannot change the colour of his skin, or a leopard remove its spots. Likewise the sinful or evil-doer cannot learn to do what is right (Jer 13:23). There is not anything good in a sinner (Rom 7:8); his understanding is darkened (Eph. 4:18; 1 Cor 2:14); his heart is deceitful (Jer 17:9-10); his mind defiled (Gen. 6:5; Tit 1:15); he is weak willed (Rom 7:18); and he is separated from God (Isa. 59:2).

The Bible explicitly states that, "The wages of sin is death" (Rom 6:23)—death which separates the soul from the Lord and from the light of life.

Sin has been the cause of agony of the ages. Indian saints in the past journeyed to Himalayan jungles searching for liberation. They lived in *tapas* (severe austerity), lived naked under the sky in severest winters, walking on fire and nails, lived on scanty food, yet lamenting or bemoaning (Rgveda 7.86.2-7).

In agony of such spiritual tension, the Vedic saints cried aloud:

Situated though I am in the midst of the waters, I am thirsty
for water. Be kind and give me rest.

(Rgveda 7.89.4)

O' Sin in my mind, why do you give me evil counsels? Get
away. I do not desire you.

(Atharva Veda 6.45.1)

From unreality lead me unto Reality,
From darkness lead me into Light;
And from death lead me unto Life-Eternal.

(Br. Ar. Up. 1.3.28)

Learned Shankaracharya cried out: Repeated birth,
repeated death and repeated lying in mother's womb–this
worldly process is too difficult to cross. Save, O' destroyer
of Mura, by your Grace (Bhaj Govindam).

Similarly, modern saints have made laborious efforts in spirit:

I have become like a blind man. O' Saviour, show me the way.

(Sant Tuka Ram)

I am feeble and lowly-full of evil thoughts. Who else can,
except my Lord, bear the punishment of my sin?

(Narayan Vaman Tilak)

Have mercy on me, O' God, according to your unfailing love.

(Ps. 51:1)

God is known as 'Father' and 'Saviour' in the Bible and
Rgveda (4.17.7). God as Father took initiative to save
mankind by taking their suffering upon Himself under the
impulse of love. This is called His vicarious suffering on
behalf of others. Nearly 2000 year ago–at a time when all
the major philosophies of religions, such as the philosophy
of Greeks, the Samkhya, the Vedanta, the Yoga, the

Hebrews, the Jain, the Buddhists, the Persian and others, had been fading and becoming ineffective in filling the Spiritual thirst of mankind–God the Father took body in the Person of the Lord Jesus Christ as *Full Incarnation*. He came in order to bear upon His Cross, once for all, the bondage or *karma-danda* of humanity (1 Jn 3:8).

After His vicarious suffering on the Cross, Jesus said, "It is finished." He died for the sins of the world and rose up again from the dead, so that men and women who come to Him for refuge may be liberated from bondage forever.

The Good News (Gospel) is "For God so loved the world that He gave his only begotten Son, that whoever believes in Him should not perish but have everlasting life." (Jn 3:16).

It is to be noted that *moksha* (release from bondage/ liberation/redemption) is not by *karma*. The Bible has stated very clearly that salvation is by grace, not by works (Eph 2:8). All our righteous deeds are like filthy rags (Isa 64:6). Good works, however desirable they may be in *dharma*, cannot be the cure of sin (Cf. Micah 6:6-7; Ezek 33:13, etc.).

If man could be saved by a meritorious act, there was no need for the self-sacrificing incarnation of God in Christ and His suffering upon the Cross.

The Bhagvad-Gita has ably developed the doctrine of the Upanishads that God does not accept *karma* good or bad (2.50; 5.15). Both (good and bad) are ineffective as far as liberation is concerned (2.50). And rebirth is always an abode of sorrow (Gita 8.15). As an alternative, Gita advocates *nishkam karma-yoga*, which means doing something without any desire for reward or merit.

The Grace of God has saving power. It has saved mankind through faith in Lord Jesus Christ (Eph. 2:8). The knowledge of God's mercy, grace and love for mankind,

His suffering on behalf of sinners and the existence of only one true God had already been given long before the incarnation of God in Jesus, between 1500-700 B.C. (Exo. 34:6; Jer 31.3; Isa 53;4-5; Isa 45:22)

The *rishis* also knew that *moksha* was obtainable by the Grace of God (Grace means unmerited favour). God the Father grants us this grace regardless of our merit or works. Such initiative of God is also well expressed in *Rgveda,* in various places. No one can find release without God's grace (Rgveda 2.28.5-6). Trembling in spirit, the devotee seeks forgiveness of Him (Rgveda 7.89.2; 2.27.5, 14; 7.86.2-7). God is called destroyer of sin (*Papnudam*) in Shvetash Vatra Up. 6.5. He reveals Himself to His chosen (Kath Up. 1.2.23). *Bhaj Govindam* of Shankara says: "Serve the Lord, O thou fool; when comes thy appointed time of death, the Rules of Grammar will surely not save you."

The entire philosophy of Shri Ramnujacharya and Shri Madhavacharya is based on the assumption that the Grace of God somehow overcomes the cycle of *karma*. So also is the *Shaiva Siddhanta.* Bhagvad-Gita also ends finally on the Grace of God as the supreme and quickest source of *moksha* in its last chapter (Gita 18.62). The Vedic saints looked to God for forgiveness of sins (Rgveda 10.133.6; 7.86.2-7; 7.89.3; 5.85.7-8, etc.)

According to the Bible, salvation is from God alone. God, the creator, became the Lamb of God to take away the sins of the world (Jn 1:29; Heb 10:5-7; Ps 40:6-8). The animal sacrifices described in the Law of Moses and in Yajur Veda can be regarded as the shadows of the perfect sacrifice made by Lord Jesus Christ on the Cross. Jesus is the sacrificial Lamb in the plan of God (Revelation 13:8; 1 Peter 1:18-19). In God's plan, Jesus fulfils the role of *Prajapati* of Rgveda who willed to become a sacrificial body to be offered by saints and who is the prime womb of creation (Rgv. 10.121; Br. Ar. Up. 1.2.7; Rgveda 10.121.10).

So, Christ Jesus is the Grace (unmerited favour) of God and God-given way for *moksha*. He is the full embodiment of God. Only He came to save the lost, only He suffered vicariously for the sin of the world and only He rose from the dead and lives as the justification of our liberation. That is why Jesus used to say, "I am the Way, the Truth and the Life, No one comes to the Father but by Me." (Jn 14:6). That is why He calls and invites: "Come unto Me all ye that are weary and heavy-laden, I will give you rest." (Matt 11:28).

The saving Grace of God is a gift of God. A sinner is saved by the grace of God through faith. Faith means that every sinner deserves death penalty as the wages of sin (Rom 6:23), but God, who is love (1 Jn 4:8, 12), could not see this suffering and dying of humanity, so His amazing love compelled Him to take back the penalty of death upon Himself on the Cross in Jesus Christ to liberate humanity from its bondage to sin. Faith in Jesus Christ—that He suffered death on the Cross on my behalf and shed his holy blood for the remission of my sin (Heb. 9:22)—and not *karma* or works will save me. Believing persons are counted righteous before God (Rom 1:17, 3:22-26; 5:1; 8:1; 2 Corin 5:17).

Many in the world have found this grace and are witness thereof. They found *joy*, *peace* and *moksha* by the grace of God in Jesus Christ, experiencing their release at the foot of the Cross.

Humanity, therefore, need not suffer any more under *maya*, *triguna* (passion, anger and greed) or *karma*, for God the Father has provided Jesus the Sadguru, for the cancellation of bondages. If there is any delay in our liberation, it is because something is wrong with us.

Moksha should be an experience of divine encounter between God and the soul, at which all darkness flees and all bondages cease. There is no question of rebirth after such an experience. This experience is self-certifying and requires no other evidence (प्रत्यक्ष प्रमाण) (Rom 8:16; Br. Ar. Up. 4.4.8). Direct experience of divine encounter is a must. Goswami Tulsi Das says, "You cannot love whom you do not know." This is very right as in the past, in their pursuit of God, people made many crude and curious images of the unknown God.

The mystic St. Bernard of Clairvaux said, "Only the lover can record how sweet it is to love the Lord!"

Shri Ramkrishna Paramhansa and his follower Swami Vivekananda were also of the view that there must be an experience of God. (Teaching of Ram Krishna p.177; Vivekananda Sahitya, Part b, p 243).

He who wants to have God-experience must have *faith to believe and courage to follow,* when the way has been shown to him.

Jesus is sin-bearer (Savour). His name, 'Jesus,' means saviour of sinners. According to Matthew 1:21, "She will have a Son, and you will name Him Jesus, because He will save His people from their sins."

Describing Eternal Life, Jesus says:

> This is Eternal Life: that they may know You, the only true God, and Jesus Christ whom You have sent (Jn 17:3).

Knowledge (*jnana*) of God and His Sent One, Jesus Christ, is the true Eternal Life. And *knowledge (jnana)* is an *experience.* Jesus further said, "I know My sheep, and My sheep know Me, as the Father knows Me and I know the Father. (Jn 10:14-15).

The Christian experience of *moksha* is the inner knowledge of his acceptance before God, the forgiveness of sins, after having realised and confessed, cancellation of bonds, the presence of inner peace and joy, happiness and the sense of belonging and abiding in the life of Christ the Lord.

The Bible says, "If the Son makes you free, you are free indeed" (Jn 8:36; 1 Jn 1:8-10; 2: 1-2) (*Fulfilment of the Vedic Quest in the Lord Jesus Christ* by Acharya Daya Prakash.)

(24) Jesus the Sin-Bearer had authority over Sin and Sickness

Jesus dispelled the darkness of sin and sickness as the Sadguru must do (Mark 2:5-12): Jesus healed a paralysed man in Capernaum of Galilee (Northern Israel). He was preaching a message in a house full of people. Four men, carrying a paralysed man, arrived. Because of the crowd they could not take the man to Jesus. So they made an opening in the roof right above the place where Jesus was. Then they let down the bed in which the paralysed man lay. Seeing their faith, Jesus said to the paralysed man, "My son your sins are forgiven." Some teachers of the Law thought to themselves. This is a blasphemy. God is the only one who can forgive sins. At once Jesus knew what they were thinking, so He said to them, "Why do you think such things? I will prove to you, then, that the Son of Man has authority on earth to forgive sins." So He said to the paralysed man, "I tell you, get up, pick up your bed and go home. He got up, took his bed and walked out in full view of them all. This amazed everyone and they praised God, saying, "We have never seen anything like this." (Mk 2:5-12).

(25) **Christ and** *Saccidananda*

The Bible holds that God is one, expressed in the triune form (the Holy Trinity) of Father, Son and Holy Spirit.

In Vedanta also, the *Paramatma* (Pra-Brahma) is usually spoken of in a *trinity of word*, such as *Saccidananda* (*Sat* [Truth] + *Chit* [Intelligence] + *Anand* [Joy]) or the trinity of *Satyam* (Truth) + *Jnanam* (Knowledge) + *Anantam* (The Infinite). Thus both scriptures have given a trinitarian name to God (*Fulfillment of Vedic Quest in the Lord Jesus Christ* by Acharya Daya Prakash).

(26) **The Eternal, Cosmic Christ**

Christ exists without a beginning and without an end (called *anadi* and *ananta*). He is the Eternal Word, beyond time and history. He is the Cosmic Logos. He is everlasting (unchanging); so He is without end or beginning.

The everlasting, cosmic or eternal Christ, who entered history at the incarnation (about 4 B.C.), left his heavenly abode, emptied Himself and brought the Kingdom of God or Kingdom of heaven on earth for mankind—as good news to the poor, to heal the broken-hearted, to announce release to the captives, and freedom to those in prison, to comfort all who mourn (Isaiah 61:1-2; Luke 4:18-19).

The incarnation of the Cosmic Christ was meant to show a great light to people who walked in darkness, for the shining of light on them who lived in a land of shadows, to give them great joy and happiness (Isaiah 9:2-3). His incarnation in history was to break the yoke that burdened them and the rod that beat their shoulders (Isa. 9:4). And when the incarnation did take place and the Sadguru started preaching by going from village to village, He said, "Repent, for the kingdom of God is at hand." He preached the kingdom of God, healed the sick, raised the dead and had full control over sin, sickness and the nature. He had all authority over heaven and on earth (Matt 28:19).

Christ is the Head and the mainstay of all truth and righteousness. He is the head of the cosmic order. He fulfils the role of *Prajapati* or *Purusha* of the Upanishads. Christ is the king of the kingdom of God. That kingdom has been defined as, "Righteousness, Peace and Joy in the Holy Spirit (Rom. 14:17).

The eternal or cosmic Christ is the visible image of the invisible God. He is pre-existent and pre-eminent in creation (Ps. 2:7; Jn 8:58; Col. 1:15-17). He is the firstborn Son, superior to all created things. For through Him God created everything in heaven and on earth, the seen and the unseen things including spiritual powers, lords, rulers and authorities. God created the whole universe through Him and for Him. Christ existed before all things, and in union with him all things have their proper place: (Col 1:15-17). According to the Gospel of John, John presents Jesus as the Eternal Word of God, who became a human being and lived among us. "Before the world was created the Word (*Shabda*) already existed; He (the Word) was with God, and He was the same as God. From the very beginning the Word was with God. Through Him God made all things; not one thing in all creation was made without him. The Word was the source of life, and this life brought light to mankind. The Word was in the world, and though God made the world through Him, the world did not recognise Him" (Jn 1:1-4, 10).

The Cosmic Christ came to be known to the world only when He came in human form as the full *and final incarnation* of the absolute (Jn 1:14; 17: 5, 24). He revealed the invisible and absolute in the visible form (Col 1:15).

Now we know what God is like, because He is like Christ. Christ said, "He who has seen Me has seen the Father" (Jn 14:9). He also said, "I and the Father are one" (Jn 10:30). Now we know that God is *righteous* and *holy* and hates sin. He is *just* and will punish evil. He is *love,* and therefore, willing to suffer to any extent for the sake of His creation. He did suffer on the Cross. God is omniscient, omnipotent and omnipresent.

The eternal or Cosmic Christ suffered on the Cross for His creation, died and rose up from the dead on the third day. He put on His spiritual body, was seen by His disciples and talked to them and ate with them after His resurrection. After His resurrection, He was seen by people whose spiritual eyes were opened. The Eternal Christ abides in the believers through the Holy Spirit whom He has sent to indwell all who are willing to unite with Him by His yoke (or *yoga*). The eternal Word of God after His resurrection went back to the place where He was before (with the Father) and from there He sent this Holy Spirit to guide and teach all truth to His disciples (Jn 6:62). This Christ is to come again visibly, just as He has ascended (Acts 1:11). He is to come again, first secretly in the air. Then he is to come visibly in His glory to eliminate sin from His creation. He will come and rule the earth for 1,000 years and discipline the nations of the earth. Finally, the earth will be renovated and God will dwell with His saints for ever. Then, there will be no more sin, no more sorrow, no more tears. God will dwell with His saints, and there will be no need of sun or moon on new earth, for the light of God will fill the universe (Revelation 22:5).

Finally, in the end, there will be only one shepherd and one flock, all united and held together in the Cosmic Christ (Eph. 1:10) (*Fulfilment of the Vedic Quest in the Lord Jesus Christ* by Acharya Daya Prakash).

(27) **Jesus the Sadguru as our Sustainer**

Jesus keeps a close watch on His saved (redeemed or liberated) ones, as the adversary of this world (Satan) tempts them in various ways. The Bible says, "Be alert, be on your watch! Your enemy, the Devil, roams round like a roaring lion, looking for some one to devour" (1 Peter 5:8). This is a regular feature of satanic activity for the people of God. For this, we have to resist Satan, then he will run away from us (James 4: 7).

Sometimes it so happens that Satan asks for God's chosen ones and receives the permission to test them as we see in Luke 22:31, 32, where Jesus tells Simon (His leading disciple) that Satan has received permission to test all of them, to separate the good from bad, as a farmer separates the wheat from the chaff. But *Jesus prayed for Simon, that his faith will not fail.* And asks him that when he turns back to Him, he must strengthen his brothers (Luke 22:31-32). Here, Jesus the Sadguru plays the role of our sustainer.

(28) **Jesus as intercessor of His disciples and would-be Disciples**

When Jesus had finished the work the Father gave Him to do on earth and He was going back to the Father, He prayed for His disciples and for those who believed in Him. He prayed for their safety, security and unity. He says, "And now I am coming to You; I am no longer in the world, but they are in the world. Holy Father keep them safe by the power of Your name, the name You gave Me, so that they may be one just as You and I are one. While I was with them, I kept them safe by the power of Your name, the name You gave me. I protected them, and not one of them was lost, except the man who was bound to be lost so that the scripture might come true. And now I am coming to You, and say these things in the world so that they might have joy in their hearts in all its fullness. I gave them Your message, and the world hated them, because they do not belong to the world, just as I do not belong to the world. I do not ask You to take them out of the world, but I do ask You to keep them safe from the Evil One...I sent them into the world, just as You sent me into the world. And for their sake I dedicate Myself to You, in order that they, too, may be truly dedicated to You.

"I Pray not only for them, but also for those who believe in Me because of their message. I pray that they may all be one. *Father!* May they be in us, just as You are in Me and I am in You. May they be one, so that the world will believe that You sent Me. I gave them the same glory You gave Me, so that they may be one, just as You and I are one : I in them and You in Me. So that they may be completely one, in order that the world may know that You sent Me and that You love them as you love Me...*Righteous Father!* The world does not know You, but I know You, and these know that You sent Me. I made You known to them, and I will continue to do so, in order that the love You have for Me may be in them, and so that I also may be in them" (Jn 17:11-26).

(29) **Jesus grants Sacrament (दीक्षा संस्कार) to His Disciples**
This sacrament or *Deeksha Samskara* is granted in the name of God the Father, God the Son and God the Holy Spirit to give new birth or born-again life (spiritual life) to the disciples.

(30) **Jesus—Teacher of Mysticism**
Mysticism has been defined as the quest of the soul for union and communion with its Creator, an experience of divine life flowing into its own.

Jesus, in reality, was teacher (Guru) of the life of the Spirit. His words were the Sprit and truth (Jn 6:63).

He taught that God and Man have to be united as branches are united with the vine. Jesus used several symbols and parables in explaining mystical truths. His mysticism was often to be observed in His solitude, silence, listening to the still voice of the heavenly Father, meditation, contemplation, communion and prayer. Very early in the morning, long before daylight, Jesus used to go out of town to a lonely place and resort to prayer (Mark 1:35).

After all the people had been baptised by John the Baptist, Jesus was also baptised. While He was praying, heaven was opened, and the Holy Spirit (the Spirit of God or God in Spirit) came down upon Him in bodily form like a dove. And a voice came from heaven, "You are My own dear Son, I am pleased with 'You.'" (Lk 3:21-22).

After His baptism, Jesus being full of the Holy Spirit was led by the Spirit into the desert, where He was tempted by the Devil for 40 days. During those days He ate nothing. He defeated the tempter. He was in His solitude, silence, prayerful atmosphere, meditation and contemplation. He was in complete union and communion with His heavenly Father. It was the full experience of the divine life flowing into own. This teaches us about the conditions suitable for mystical truths, knowledge and experience of inward flowing of the Spirit of God.

(31)Jesus taught the scriptures with authority (Mt 7:28-29)

His authority over scriptures is seen when he concluded the 'Sermon on the Mount'; the crowds were amazed at his teaching, because He taught as one who had authority, and not as their teachers of the law.

(32) Risen Christ—interpreter of His own death

He interpreted it according to the Scriptures. "And beginning from Moses and from all the prophets He interpreted to the disciples in all the scriptures the things concerning Himself." He never offered any other interpretation. There is no other. St. Paul reminds the Corinthians how he delivered unto them first of all that which he had received, how Christ died for our sins according to the scriptures.

Views of some great men about Jesus the Sadguru

"A man who was completely innocent, offered himself as a sacrifice for the good of others, including his enemies, and became the ransom of the world. It was a perfect act."

– Mahatma Gandhi

"Jesus was the first socialist, the first to seek a better life for mankind"

– Mikhail Gorbachev (former Prime Minister of USSR).

"I really do not know what will remain of civilization and history if the accumulated influence of Christ, both direct and indirect, is eradicated from literature, art, practical dealings, moral standards and creativeness in the different activities of mind and spirit."

–Charles Malik (Lebanon), Former President of U.N. General Assembly.

"The Religious Truth is found in Plato and Upanishads. Its embodiment is found in the life of Jesus."

–Dr. S. Radhakrishnan

"If Hinduism be defined as the relentless pursuit of truth, and if Christ is indeed the truth, it is inevitable that they belong to each other."

–Swami Shilananda (an Indian Christian).

"Gandhiji commented,'I shall tell the Hindus: Your lives will be incomplete unless you reverently study the teachings of Jesus.'"

(Reported in the *Message of Christ*, Bombay, 1963, p. 42)

"Christ was related to all the other faiths as fulfilment. I saw Christ gathering up all these scattered truths within Himself and completing and perfecting them. I could, therefore, be the friend of truth anywhere."

–Acharya E. Stanley Jones,'*Along the Indian Road*

"I am feeble and lowly, full of evil thoughts. Who else can, except my Lord (Jesus), bear the punishment of my sin?"

– Narayan Vaman Tilak (a Christian poet)

"Jesus is the radiance of God's glory and the exact representation of His being, sustaining all things by His powerful word (Heb 1:3); He is the Power and Wisdom of God (1 Cor 1 : 24); He is the image of the invisible God (Col 1:15); He is the mystery of God (Col 2:2); He is the Son of God (Rom 1:4); He is the Will of God the Father to finish His work (Jn 4:34)

– St Paul (an Apostle of Christ)

Part II

Disciples and Discipleship of Jesus the Sadguru

CHAPTER 5

Different Leaders and their Disciples

Generally, the followers of a teacher or guru are known as disciples. So, the Guru must have disciples to follow him. The disciples look to the Guru for receiving redemption from their fallen state of bondage and sorrow.

(a) Moses had disciples (Jn. 9:28)

(b) John the Baptist had disciples (Jn 1:35; Mt 9:14; Acts 19:1-5)

(c) The Pharisees had disciples (Luke 5:33; Mark 2:18)

(d) False teachers also want to have disciples (Acts 20:30)

(e) An Acharya (assistant teacher or Up-guru) selects his disciples (*Satyakam* in Chandogya Upanishad 4.4.1)

(f) Jesus had disciples (Jn 2:2; 15:16)

(a) **Moses, the Lawgiver, had Disciples**
God gave Law through Moses (Jn 1: 17). The Pharisees (the religious leaders of the Jews) regarded Moses as their Guru, as God would speak with Moses face to face (Exo 3:1-22; 4:1-17; 33:11; Deut 18:14-19; Jn 9:28, etc.)

(b) **John the Baptist had Disciples**
He was a Judean relative of Jesus, who had grown up as an ascetic living in the Judean desert. He was the forerunner

of the Lord Jesus Christ. He was God's messenger sent before Jesus Christ, to clear the way for Jesus' ministry. He appeared in the desert, baptising (giving water sacrament or *jal samskara*) and preaching. He told the people to turn away from their sins and be baptised, and God will forgive their sins. Many people from the province of Judea and the city of Jerusalem went to hear John. They confessed their sins, and John baptised them in the river Jordan (Mark 1:2-5).

John the Baptist, introduced Jesus to the Public and to his disciples saying Jesus was the Lamb of God who takes away the sin of the world (Jn 1:29) And he further said, "I tell you that He (Jesus) is the Son of God." (Jn 1:34-37).

(c) The Pharisees had Disciples (Luke 5:33)

Of the three prominent sects of Judaism during the days of Christ, such as the Pharisees, Sadducees and Essenes, the Pharisees were by far the most influential. This sect was the most strict sect of the Jews (Acts 26:5). There was, however, a group of Jews resembling the Pharisees as far back as the Babylonian captivity (605-539BC).

The Pharisees were known as "separated ones, separatists" (from 135 BC) and known as "loved of God" or "loyal to God." They were found everywhere in Palestine; their highest number never exceeded 6,000; and they wore a distinguishable garb so as to be easily recognised. They became a closely organised group and were very loyal to the society and to each other, but separate from others, even from their own people. They were highly respected by the Jewish people and were highly faithful to the law. They pledged themselves to obey all the facets of the traditions to the minutest detail, and were sticklers for ceremonial purity. They paid tithe in addition to the temple tax. They had no association with tax-collectors, with people who had been defiled through sickness. In fact, they had made life difficult for themselves and bitter for others. They despised those whom they did not consider their equal and were haughty and arrogant because they believed they were the only interpreters of God and His word. Being people of the law, they believed in the final reward for good works and that the souls of the wicked were detained for ever under the earth, while those of the virtuous, rose again and even migrated into other bodies. They despised Herods (the kings) and Romans (the ruling power); they hated Jesus' doctrine of equality and claims of messiahship with equal fervour (Jn 9:16, 22).

Their teaching and their concept of religion was the belief that the Babylonian exile of 70 years (605 to 539BC) was caused by Israel's failure to keep the *Torah* (The Mosaic Law), and that its keeping was an individual as well as a national duty.

The Pharisees had disciples who used to fast frequently and offer prayers (Luke 5:33). Jesus spoke to His twelve followers first, to be on guard against the yeast (hypocrisy) of the Pharisees (Luke 12:1). Jesus condemned especially their ostentation, their hypocrisy, their salvation by works, their impenitence or self-righteousness and lovelessness but not always Pharisees as such. Some of the great men of NT were Pharisees, such as Necodemus (Jn 3:1), Gamaliel (Acts 5:34) and Paul (Acts 26:5; Phil 3:5). Some of the Pharisees were members of the Christian movement in the beginning (Acts 6:7).

(d) False Teachers want to have Disciples
Paul meets with the leaders of the church of Ephesus and tells them all the truth about God, and warns them to keep a careful watch over themselves and over the church–God had bought the church with His own blood (Acts 20:30; 2

pet 2:1-3, 10, 15-18). And says, "Yes I know that when I am
gone, hungry wolves will come in among you. They will
try to destroy the church. Also men from your own group
(false teachers) will begin to teach things that are not true.
They will get men to follow them" (Acts 20:30; 2 Peter 2:1-
3, 10, 15-16).

(e) Acharya Selects his Disciples

The role of the disciple or *brahmachari* in the East has always
been of a learner and obedient server of the Master (*Swami*,
teacher, or *Acharya*). The *brahmachari* (disciple) would
clean and prepare the *ashram* and be willing to be sent out
to bring water, fuel and food. It was the same in the case
of the disciples of Jesus. (Satya Kam in Chandogya Up.
4.41.)

CHAPTER 6

Disciples of Jesus

Jesus had disciples (Jn 2:2; 15:16). He chose and appointed them to bear the fruit that endures (Jn 15:16). His first-called disciples were mostly fishermen (Mt 4:18-22; Lk 5:1-11; Mk 1:16-20; Jn 1:40). His first public ministry, with those few disciples, was in the Jordon valley and focused on Baptism (Jn 3:22). Jesus appeared as the second Baptist.

After this, Jesus withdrew to His own region of Galilee and started there itinerant preaching and healing in synagogues and houses. Mark 1:29-34 gives a picture of preaching and healing in Peter's house, where all the people of the town had gathered in front of the house.

Soon Jesus' name, fame and glory spread far and wide, and the scriptures (Mk 3:7-12) say that, by the lake of Galilee, a large crowd followed Jesus (from Galilee, Judea, Jerusalem, Idumea, Jordon, cities of Tyre and Sidon) to hear and to be healed even by touching Him. The crowd was so large that Jesus told His disciples to get a boat ready for Him in order to avoid being crushed (Mk 3:7-12).

Jesus had many disciples (Luke 6:17). The 'crowds' came and went, listening to Jesus eagerly, but not committed to follow Him; the *disciples* were those who to a greater or lesser degree threw in *their lot* with Him and accompanied Him on His travels.

Jesus Chooses Twelve Apostles

At that time Jesus went up a hill to pray and spend the whole night there praying to God. When the day came, He called His disciples to Him and chose twelve of them, whom He named apostles. *Simon* (whom He named Peter) and his brother *Andrew;* James and John, Philip and Bartholomew, Matthew and Thomas, James, son of Alphaeus, and Simon (who was called Zealot or Patriot), Judas son of James, and Judas Iscariot, who became the traitor (Lk 6:12-16; Mt 10:1-4).

Jesus Teaches and Heals

When Jesus had come down from the hill with twelve apostles, He stood on a level place with a large number of His disciples. A large crowd of people was there from all over Judea, from Jerusalem and from coastal cities of Tyre and Sidon; they had come to hear Him and to be healed of their diseases. Those who were troubled by evil spirits also came and were healed. All the people tried to touch Him, for power was going out from Him and healing them all (Lk 6:17-19; Mt 4:23-25).

Sermon on the Mount

This Sermon is recorded beautifully in Matthew chapters 5, 6 and 7. Its teaching is applicable to all people of all ages. The Sermon on the Mount is Christ's instruction to us for godly living in the present world. It is applicable to literally all humans.

In Mathew chapters 5, 6 and 7, Jesus touches every important aspect of life and instructs how to live in this world and prepare ourselves for entering the kingdom of God.

A majority of the disciples were Galileans. Of the inner circle of 12, most of them were from Galilee. But they were different in character and background as Thomas was a pessimist type, Peter was an extrovert, active and leader type, Matthew, being a Tax-Collector, was pro-Roman government employer, Simon 'The Zealot' was a patriot; and John and James were known as sons of thunder. Jesus taught all these people humility and the secret of becoming greatest of all by being servant of all, by His teaching and, practically, by washing their feet. These apostles were made the foundation of the world's greatest religion. And Jesus Himself became the cornerstone. Jesus' complete love for them and His new commandment to love one another, even as He had loved them (Jn 13:34-35) and his intercessory prayer (Jn chapter 17) made them humble and united them in oneness.

Jesus Sends out the Twelve Disciples for Limited Ministry

Jesus called his twelve apostles (disciples) and gave them authority over all demons—to cast them out and to heal every disease and infirmity. He charged them to go to the lost sheep of the house of Israel. And preach as they go, saying, "The kingdom of heaven is at hand" (Mt 10:1, 7).

The apostles had been in the company of Jesus as He travelled around the Galilean countryside proclaiming the good news of the kingdom, healing every disease and affliction (Mt 9:35). Now Jesus was sending them out as His ambassadors to gain first-hand experience as missionaries. In commissioning them, He empowered them to heal as He had healed, to cast out demons as He had cast them out, to proclaim, as He had, that the kingdom of God was at hand (Mt 10:1,7).

These disciples were quite ordinary men, economically, academically and socially, chosen by Jesus to carry on His work. These were the disciples, who after Jesus' ascension, after the coming of the Holy Spirit at Pentecost, preached and baptised 3,000 people (Acts 2:41) and remained faithful to their calling, did not stop teaching and preaching Jesus as the Christ, despite the persecutions they endured (5:42).

Take a look at Matthew 10:8-15. Jesus says, "Heal the sick, raise the dead, cleanse lepers, cast out demons...." It is clear from Jesus' words that the apostles were to be totally reliant on God and His goodness and generosity. There was to be confidence in the power of the gospel to change lives, to heal, to purify (Mt 10:8). There was certainly urgency about the mission. It was not to be delayed on account of proper arrangement of things (Mt 10:9, 10). Nothing was to distract them from their mission. Subsistence, but not profit, was to be their expectation. Preaching the gospel was not to be a business, and it would not be accepted by all. Where it was rejected, the response was not to be condemnation or a desire for retribution; it was a symbolic shaking of the dust from their feet (Mt 10:14).

So, Jesus wants the disciples to be totally reliant on God and His goodness and generosity. Such an attitude recognises God as a loving and personal Father who will always faithfully provide for His people and will never abandon them. Such a loving Father will sustain us as well. We can only have a true missionary's heart when we trust in God and are convinced of His generosity and faithfulness.

Take a look at Matthew 10:16-23. "Behold, I send you out as sheep in midst of wolves....you will be hated by all for My name's sake...before the Son of Man comes."...The early (primitive) Church experienced persecution from both Jews and Gentiles. Despite this, Jesus told His apostles that He was sending them out "as sheep in the midst of wolves" (Mt 10:16). He warned them that it would not be easy to follow Him and be His disciples. They would be persecuted at times even by their own families who would be devoid of love for them and for Jesus as well. They would have to be patient till end.

Truly, the way of discipleship was not going to be easy, but Jesus did not leave them defenseless. He promised that the Holy Spirit would be with them, teaching them and guiding them in every situation. Jesus knew that if they were true to Him and to His teaching, they would be "wise as serpents and innocent as doves" (Mt 10:16). Innocent as dove signifies that they would be free from judgment and anger by the power of Christ's transforming love.

Take a look at Matthew 10:24-33. "A disciple is not above his teacher, nor a servant above his master; it is enough for the disciple to be like his teacher, the servant like his master...have no fear of them...I will also deny before My Father who is in heaven..." Jesus' call to His disciples was a call (first and foremost) to become like Him. When He called Andrew and Simon Peter, He told them that He would make them fishers of men (Mt 4:19). By following Him, they would be transformed into His likeness. Jesus' heart would become theirs, like their master; they would long for the day when all people would hear the good news and accept the gospel message.

Jesus also warned His disciples that sharing in the life of the master is not without its challenges and difficulties: "If they have called the master of the house Beelzebub, how much more will they malign those of His household" (Mt 10:25). At the same time, Jesus repeatedly told them not to be afraid of what happens to them (Mt 10:26, 28, 31). They should rather fear God who has authority and power over their body and soul as well (Mt 10:1-33; *Matthew: A devotional commentary* by Fr. J.A. Minding, pp 88-93).

Take a look at Luke 10:1-11 (sending out of 70 other disciples; also, for limited Ministry). "After this the Lord chose 70 others. He sent them 2 by 2 to every city and place where He was to go (or would be going later). Jesus said to them," There is much grain (crop) ready to gather. But the workmen are few. Pray to the Lord who is the owner of the grain fields (harvest) that He will send workmen to gather His grain. Go on your way. Listen, I send you like lambs among wolves. Take no money. Do not take a bag or shoes. Speak to no one along the way. When you go to a house say, peace be to this house. And if the son of peace be there, your peace shall rest upon it: if not, it shall return to you again. And in the same house remain, eating and drinking such things as they give: for the labourer is worthy of his hire. Go not from house to house.

"And into whatever city you enter, and they receive you, eat such things as are set before you: And heal the sick that are therein, and say unto them, the kingdom of God is at hand. But into whatever city you enter, and they receive you not, go your ways out into the streets of the same city, and say, Even the very dust of your city, which cleaves on us, we do wipe off against you: notwithstanding be you sure of this, that the kingdom of God is come nigh unto you."

Let's take a look at Lk 10:17-20. Then the 70 returned with joy, saying. "Lord, even the demons are subject to us in your name. And He said to them, I saw Satan fall like lightning from heaven. Behold, I give you the authority to trample on serpents and scorpions, and over all power of enemy, and nothing shall by any means hurt you. Nevertheless do not rejoice in this, that spirits are subject to you, but rather rejoice because your names are written in heaven."

The apostles' mission is not an exclusive one. Those who are baptised (have received the *deeksha samskara* granted by the Guru, Jesus), too are commissioned to follow in the footsteps of Jesus and preach the message of redemption or salvation. Like the apostles, they are empowered by the Holy Spirit to proclaim the good news of Jesus Christ. Jesus shed his blood for the world. Blood has life. By giving or donating ordinary blood to a sick person, he gets healed. The Holy blood shed by Jesus was for the redemption of our sins, sinful nature and cancellation of our bondage to sin and sorrow. Those who believe this action of the only Holy blood of Jesus are saved by grace through faith (Eph. 2:8). This has to be preached by all the disciples of this age.

If we are faithful to our calling as ministers of Christ's word, the Gospel will be spread and God's kingdom will be built. Today, let all the called people and all clergy (ordained to serve Lord Jesus) know Jesus' life and power more deeply as they proclaim the gospel.

In the passages quoted above, Matthew and Luke provide guidance to the Jewish community and other Christian communities on the call of discipleship. As Matthew was recalling Jesus' instructions to the twelve disciples (when Jesus sent them out on their first missionary journey), Matthew was fully aware of the Great Commission that applies to all believers: "Go therefore, and make disciples of all nations" (Mt 28:19). The mission given by Jesus to His disciples was unique, yet as baptised Christians, we too participate in Jesus' Great Commission.

The early church was persecuted by both Jews and Gentiles. Likewise the present church can experience ridicule, rejection, harassment and timidity while going out among wolves (Mt 10:16-18). But our protection and wisdom will come from the Holy Spirit as we seek God through prayer, scripture reading and hearing the voice of the Lord. If our minds are filled with the truth of God's Word, we will have the strength and the knowledge to withstand those who oppose Christ and His way of life.

Jesus' call to His disciples continues to be a call, (first and foremost), to become like Him. He wants His disciples to become fishers of men. Because we are members of Jesus' body, we all have to share His victory over the evil one (Satan). But it also implies that the devil's temptations remain a part of all disciples' lives in this world. In any case, the disciple need not succumb, however fierce the attack may seem, or however weak we may feel. Our Master–Lord Jesus Christ–is in us to comfort and strengthen us. He is our wisdom and will give us all we need as we turn to Him in humble faith (Mt 10:19-20). Let the disciples not lose heart, for He who is in us is greater than he who is in the world (1 Jn 4:4).

Women who Followed Jesus

They were *Mary* (who was called Magdalene), from whom seven demons had been driven out; *Joanna,* whose husband Chuza was an officer in Herod's Court; *Susanna*; and many other women who used their own resources to help Jesus and His disciples (Lk 8:1-3).

CHAPTER 7

Requirements for Being a Disciple of the Sadguru

Here is a list of requirements for being a true disciple of Jesus the Sadguru.

(1) **Obedience (Jn 14:15).**
Jesus said, "If you love Me, keep My commandments."

(2) **Faithfulness (Jn 15:8)**
Jesus said, "By this My Father is glorified, that you bear much fruit; so you will be My disciples."

(3) **Abiding in His Word—Perseverance (Jn 8:31)**
Then Jesus said to those Jews who believed Him, "If you abide in My Word, you are My disciples."

(4) **Humility (Mt 10:24-25)**
"A disciple is not above his teacher, nor a servant above his master. If they have called the master of the house 'Beelzebub' how much more will they call those of His house hold."

(5) **Abiding in Jesus (Jn 15:5; Mt 11:29; 1 Jn 3:6)**
The Sadguru express very clearly, "I am the vine; you are the branches. If a man remains in Me and I in him, he will

bear much fruit; apart from me you can do nothing." (Jn 15:5). The blood of Jesus Christ cleanses us from all sin. This cleansing takes place through faith (what happens is like the story of the brazen serpent mentioned in Jn 3:14). "The Atonement and the Blood which washes us from our sins means that we are grafted into Christ, I in Him and He in me. The branch which is grafted into the tree is bitter, but once it is engrafted the sweet sap of the tree flows into the branch and makes it sweet" (said by Sadhu Sunder Singh).

(6) Abiding in Jesus' Love
Read Jn 13:34-35; 14:21; 15:9; 13:13-15; 1 Jn 4: 12, 16; 1 Jn 3:6; Judg 2:18 cf Exo 6: 2-8; 12: 40-41; 13: 20-21).

(7) Jesus Demands Complete Obedience from His Disciples
He says, "You are My friends, if you do what I command" (Jn 15:14).This is applicable to all. (cf James 2:23 Abraham is called friend of God for his obedience.)

At one time, because of His strict teaching, many followers left His company (Jn 6: 53-66); He gave option to His circle saying, "Do you also want to leave Me?" At such a solemn and serious situation, the disciples stood firm for their Guru and said, "Lord to whom shall we go? You have the words of Eternal life" (Jn 6:66-68). Such a profound commitment is rare today to find.

(8) Discipleship be Confessed Openly
Many of the Jewish authorities believed in Jesus; but because of the Pharisees they did not talk about it openly, so as not to be expelled from the synagogues. They loved the approval of men rather than the approval of God (Jn 12:42-43; Lk 9:26-27; Mt 10:32-33).

(9) Acceptance of Lifestyle of Jesus

To be a disciple involves an unreserved and total surrender (exclusive commitment) to Jesus. But for the *inner circle,* the acceptance of Jesus' lifestyle is a must, which includes a readiness to suffer persecution and exclusion from society (ostracism) for His sake (Mt 10:16-39).

Jesus and His disciples lived on the contributions and hospitality of those who supported His mission (Lk 8:3; 10:38-42; Mt 10:8-11). He taught them to rely on God *for all material needs* (Mt 6:24-30); (Mk 10:17-22). Their money was held in common (Jn 12:6; 13:29), but it sufficed only for their basic needs. *Poverty,* for Jesus, was not a disaster (Lk 6:20, 24; Mk 10:23-31). Unmarried and with no settled home (Lk 9:58) or material ties, He was free to travel around Palestine preaching and healing. The inner circle had to be free like their Guru.

In the early part of His ministry, He was invited to speak in synagogues as visiting teacher (Mk 1:21, 39; Mt 9:35; Lk 4:16-27), but later synagogue teaching is not mentioned (as His radical teaching was not acceptable) and Jesus is found teaching the crowds in the open air, and devoting more time to the instructions of His closest disciples.

Disciples are Salt of the Earth and Light of the World

The Guru demands a salt-like quality from His disciples (Mt 5:13). Salt makes food tastier and preserves it. Likewise His followers have to witness to the truth and sustain it. In other words, the mixing and association of the disciples with their respective society must have the flavour of the gospel truth making life of the earth spiritual, worth loving and worth enjoying, and approved by men and God as well.

Further, the disciples have to be the light of the world (Mt 5:14). The true light of the world is Jesus, the Sadguru

(Jn 8:12), so the disciples walking in light of their Guru have to reflect this light to the world. Their light has to enlighten the darker areas of human beings. They have to proclaim to the people still searching in the realm of spiritualism (relying upon their own words and deeds, worshipping many gods) that the act of *moksha* has been fulfilled in the cosmic Christ. Disciples should enlighten the seekers of truth that Vedanta has cultivated the soil of the heart and soul of man, and Christ has brought the seed of Truth and Life; the Holy Spirit pours the water on it. If given proper response, the flower will bloom.

It is Christ who fulfils the search of India. The Church herself finds her fulfilments in Christ who is the Head of the body.

The Church should not only share with others the life and truth she has discovered in her Lord, but should also receive with gladness what our country has to share with her. The Bible says, "The kings of the earth will bring their glory and honour into it" (Rev. 21:24).

Dr. E. Stanley Jones, the founder Acharya of Sat-tal Ashram, paid attention to *five* living seeds in Hinduism (spirit as ultimate reality; unity in the whole universe; justice at the heart of the universe; passion for freedom (liberation); and discipleship).These values must be preserved. As it spread, Christianity took many ideas from the culture of the Greeks, of the Romans and of others. There is much here in this land that can be brought into the service of the Lord. For this, the disciples have to walk in the light of their Sadguru, that is, Jesus (Jn 8:12), and then reflect the light into all these worth-knowing and useful areas of our land. True disciples are *sons of the light* and *sons of the Day* (1 These 5:2-5).

CHAPTER 8

Deny Yourself, Take Up Your Cross and Follow Me

After Peter's confession of Christ as the Son of the living God and Messiah (Mt 16: 13-16; Mk 8:27-29; Lk 9:18-20), we see the beginning of a new emphasis in Jesus' ministry. Instead of teaching the crowds in parables, He concentrated on preparing the disciples for His coming suffering and death. But Peter never wanted his Guru to suffer and die, so Jesus had to rebuke Peter for having in mind such things of men which are not of God (Mt 16:21-23; Mk 8:31-33; Lk 9:22-27).

Then Jesus said to His disciples, "If anyone would come after Me, he must deny himself and take up his cross and follow Me. For whoever wants to save his life will lose it, but whoever loses his life for Me will find it" (Mt 16:24-25; Lk 14:27; 17:33).

This call of Jesus includes the three conditions that are to be met in order to be called His disciple in the true sense. These conditions are: (i) denying of self, (ii) taking up the Cross, and (iii) following Him.

(1) Denying of Self

Jesus wants the disciple to cease to make self the object of his life and actions. Man by nature loves self. Jesus wants

His disciple to surrender and forsake all that he has (Mt 10: 37-38). Jesus said to a large crowd following Him, "Whoever comes to Me cannot be My disciple, unless he loves Me more than he loves his father and his mother, his wife and his children, his brothers and his sisters, and himself as well. Whoever does not carry his own cross and come after Me cannot be my disciple" (Lk 14 :25-27 ; Mt 10:37-38). "Whoever of you does not forsake all that he has cannot be my disciple" (Lk 14:33).

According to brother Zac Poonen, self-life leads to corruption–man's total depravity, self-centredness, 'self-centred' attitude to God, un-teachability, 'self-centred' attitude to fellowmen, pride, condemnation of others, lovelessness and so on.

Man's Total Depravity
The Bible says that the human heart is deceitful above all things and desperately wicked (Jer 17:9). It refers to every child of Adam.

St. Paul recognised that no good thing dwelt in his flesh (Rom 7:18). This was his first step to freedom (Rom 8:2).

Men look on the outward appearance and call some good and others bad. But God who looks at the heart sees all men in the same condition. The Bible (Rom 3:10-12) says, "There is none righteous, no, not one. There is none that understands, there is none that seeks after God. They are all gone out of the way, they are together become unprofitable. There is none that does good, no, not one."

Self-Centredness
Adam was created to be centred in God. The day he refused that centre and chose to be centred in himself by eating of the tree that God had forbidden–he died, as God had said

he would (Gen 3:1-19). Likewise, if our Christian life and service center in ourselves, we shall experience spiritual death. We shall be unwittingly ministering spiritual death to others too.

People wishing to be with Jesus and serve Him, must recognise the evil within. The suppression of the evil is not a victory. One person may explode in anger immediately (outwardly) while another, in a similar situation, may boil inwardly (without any expression). In men's eyes, the second person may be considered meek. But in God's eyes (who sees and knows the hearts) both men are equally bad. Jesus was aware of this, so He demands self-denial.

The 'Self-Centred' Attitude to God
Self-centred life serves God seeking a reward–spiritual blessings, material blessings, reputation, an impression of spirituality in the eyes of others, power and position in the Church and society, but it is always a legalistic service (*karm-kandi seva*), they serve for wages and want to be rewarded on their self-centred methods ignoring God's Way (Mt 20 : 1-16). God has no pleasure in legalistic service (Deut 28:47).

A self-Centred Person is not Teachable
He is so sure of his ability that he is unwilling to accept correction.

'Self–Centred' Attitude to fellow Men
A self-centred individual has jealousy and love of honour in his or her heart. Jealousy is one of the characteristics of self-centred life. Cain was jealous of the fact that Abel had been accepted by God and that he himself had been rejected (Gen 4:3-5). King Saul was jealous of young David because the women sang, "Saul has slain thousands while David has slain ten thousands" (1 Sam 18:6-7). From that day he determined to kill David.

A self-centred person loves to be noticed by others. He loves the praises of men. A self-centred Christian leader hinders the spiritual growth of those to whom he ministers, for he draws people not to Christ but to himself.

Pride

A self-centred person has a high opinion of himself. Pride is the root of all fall. It was because of pride that Lucifer (the anointed Cherub) had a great fall. He compared himself with other angels and felt that he was wiser, more beautiful and more exalted than them all. Then this anointed Cherub became the Devil. One may be like an angel, but pride can turn him or her into a devil.

On the other hand, Daniel, the prophet, was not self-centred. This holy man of God had insight, intelligence and outstanding wisdom from God' (Dan 5:11). He refused any encashment for interpreting *the writing on the wall* to King Belshazzar (Dan 5:16-17). Also, he never expected any honour, gifts or position from Nebuchadnezzar for telling and interpreting his dream (Dan, chapter 2). However, Daniel was honoured as the third highest ruler in the kingdom by King Belshazzar (Dan 5:29). King Nebuchadnezzar placed him in a high position and made him ruler over the entire province of Babylon. He made him in charge (chief) of all its wise men (Dan 2:48).

Condemnation and Lovelessness

A self-centred person does not have any real love for his fellowmen and that is why his attitude towards them is hard. For example, in the parable of Luke 15, the elder son had never tried to go and search for his lost brother. He did not care whether his brother was dead or alive. He was interested only in making merry with his friends (Lk 15:29).

We need to have the compassion of Jesus to love an unbeliever and a back slider like the young, prodigal son (Gal 6:1; 1 Jn 5:16). We must not forget that love is the greatest of the three abiding virtues (1 Cor 13:13).

Let's take a look at the overcoming of self-centredness as exemplified by Jesus and the Power of the Holy Spirit.

Jesus the Sadguru, sets the best example of His own life to make us understand self-denial or self-less life as mentioned by Paul in Phil 2 :3-11 (cf Lk 14:7-11).

"Let your attitude be the same as that of Christ Jesus (Mt 11:29) who being God (Jn 1:1) did not consider equality with God (Jn 5:18), something to be grasped, but made Himself nothing (2 Cor 8:9), taking the very nature of a servant (Mt 20:28), being made in human likeness (Jn 1:14). And being found in appearance as a man (Heb 2:9), He humbled Himself and became obedient to death (Mt 26:49)–even death on a cross! Therefore, God exalted Him to the highest place and gave Him the name that is above every name (Isa 52:13 ; Mt 28: 18; Acts 2:33; Eph 1:21; Heb 1:4-5), that in the name of Jesus every knee should bow (Ps 95:6; Isa 45:23; Rom 14:11) in heaven and on earth and under the earth (Mt 28 :18; Eph 1:10; Col 1:20) and every tongue should confess that Jesus Christ is Lord (Jn 13:13; Rom 14:9) to the glory of God the Father."

Though Jesus was God, He took the form of a servant. He washed the feet of His disciples at the last supper (Jn 13:13-15; 34-35). He said to His disciples, "If I being your Guru and Lord washed your feet, you must also wash each other's feet. He advised His disciples, not to be jealous, but love everyone without counting the cost (Mt 10:24-25; Jn 13:35; Mt 5:21-48). He died on the Cross obeying His Father's Will (Ps 40: 6-8; Heb 10:5-7; Mt 26:39; Deut 6:6).

Self-denial involves renunciation (*sanyas*). A disciple is not greater than his master (Guru). Moses, Sadhu Sundar Singh, Kartar Singh, St. Francis of Assisi and many Christian mystics did the same.

A man exists between two forces (his self-life and the Holy Spirit), which are constantly fighting each other to win control over us (Gal 5:17). Let us all bear in mind that out of many works of the Holy Spirit (Jn 16 : 5-15; 14 :15-19), His primary or Chief Ministry is to help us to put to death the deeds of the flesh (the self-life; Gal 5: 19-21).

The Bible says: "If you live after the flesh, you will die, but if you through the spirit put to death the deeds of the flesh, you will live–for as many as are led by the spirit are the Sons of God (Rom 8 : 13-14).

So, the disciples have to overcome their self-centredness by having the mind or attitude of their Sadguru, that is, Jesus (Phil 2:5-9) as well as by the power of the Holy Spirit (Rom 8 : 13-14), which was found in many followers.

(2) Taking up the Cross

(a) The Cross of Jesus

Jesus was condemned like a criminal and scourged with a whip with leather thongs, which greatly weakened Him. He was then made to carry the Cross to the scene of His torture and death (at mount Calvary). He was striped naked and was nailed to the Cross beam (Jn 20:25). There the condemned man was left to die of hunger and exhaustion. A spear was thrust into his side to make sure of death. This method of crucifixion was the most cruel and degrading form of punishment.

Theologically, the word 'Cross' was used to describe the gospel of salvation—that Jesus 'died for our sins.' So the 'preaching of the gospel' is 'the Word of the Cross,' 'the preaching of Christ crucified' (1 Cor 1:17). So the apostle glorifies 'in the Cross of our Lord Jesus Christ,' and speaks of suffering persecution 'for the Cross of Christ'. Clearly the word 'Cross' here stands for the whole glad announcement of our redemption through the atoning (substitutionary) death of Jesus.

'The word of the cross' is also the `word of reconciliation' (2 Cor 5:19). It is `through the Cross' that God has reconciled Jews and Gentiles, abolishing the middle wall of partition, the law of commandments (Eph 2:14-16). It is `by the blood of His cross' that God has made peace, in reconciling `all the things to Himself' (Col 1:20). This reconciliation is at once personal and cosmic. Christ set aside the bond which stood against us, nailing it to the cross (Col 2:14).

The Cross is a symbol of shame and humiliation and of God's wisdom and glory revealed through it. Rome used it not only as an instrument of torture and execution, but also as a shameful example reserved for the worst and lowest.

To the Jews, it was a sign of being accursed (Deut 21:23; Gal 3:13). This was the death Jesus died. He 'endured the cross, despising the shame' (Heb 12:2; Phil 2:8). Jesus gave so much importance of carrying the cross to His hearers that three times He spoke of the road of discipleship through cross-bearing (Mt 10:38; Mk 8 : 34; Lk 14 : 27).

Further, the Cross is a symbol of our union with Christ, not simply in virtue of our following His example, but in virtue of what He has done for us and in us. In His substitutionary death for us on the Cross, We died in Him (cf, 2 Cor 5:14), and 'our old man (old nature) is crucified with Him,' that by His indwelling spirit we might walk in newness of life (Rom 6:4; Gal 2:20; 5:24; 6:14), in Him.'

Christ (as the Word of God) and His Cross (as the way of redemption) were always in the heart of God from the beginning of the World (Rev. 13:8; 1 Pet 1: 20; cf Gita 3.10). And the redemption of mankind by means of Christ's crucifixion was the will of God (Ps. 40:8; Heb 10:7), which Jesus had voluntarily accepted centuries before His full and final incarnation (Ps 40:6-8; Heb 10:5-9; Heb 1:1-3). So Christ overshadows throughout the Old Testament scriptures in some way or the other (e.g. Christ is seen in Messianic prophesy as Saviour, in people and events that serve as types, as the suffering Messiah who would die on the cross to pay the penalty of mankind's' sins (Isa 53:1-12; 1 Pet 3:18; Ps 34:20; Jn 19:33, etc.) and who would finally attain the enthronement (Ps 96-99) as King-Judge-Priest, etc.

The willful sacrifice of Jesus (Jn 6:38; 1 Jn 3:8; Jn 10:11, 17) was remedy for sins (Jn 1:29; 1 Pet 1:18-19, etc.). The shadows of this real sacrifice on the Cross are seen in the Old Testament animal scarifies and Yajur Veda as well. The Cross had a great saving power even in about 1446-1445 BC when Moses lifted a brazen snake (a type of coming cross) in the wildness, all those who believed in this type of cross were saved (Numbers 21:9; Jn 3:14-15).

(b) Taking up our Daily Cross
This idea can be understood in the following manner:

(i) Taking up or carrying the daily cross is a hard and difficult way of life (of disciples) entering through a small-narrow gate and going through a narrow road leading to life (Mt 7:14).

It is to accept and obey the call of Jesus faithfully to continue His mission of love and mercy. The Cross is the same for the disciple as for Jesus, the Sadguru, who accepted and obeyed faithfully His Father's will (Ps 40:8; Heb 10:7; Isa 53:10). Discipleship is to put the will of God before all earthly ties; it is to be prepared for hardship and sacrifice; and it must place all gifts and all possessions at the disposal of the divine will. All affections, all programmes and all possessions must come under the voluntary surrender to the will of God. The disciple needs to be prepared to face a life of betrayal, a life of condemnation to death, a life of being mocked, to be flogged and crucified. Finally, discipleship is a death–march to eternal life.

The Cross was the will of God the Father for God the Son Jesus (Heb 10:7, Ps 40:8). Likewise the Cross is the call and will of Jesus the Sadguru, for His disciples (Mt 10:38). The power of God is manifested only in and through the Cross. It is in human weakness (broken condition) that the wisdom and power of God is seen (1 Cor 1:23-24; 2 Cor 13:4).

(ii) Taking up the Cross is having a fellowship with Christ as seen in the life of St. Paul. He says I have been crucified with Christ and I no longer live, but Christ lives in me. The life I live in the body, I live by faith in the Son of God (Jesus); who loved me and gave Himself for me. (Gal 2: 20)

It is only when the "I" (the self-life) is crucified and surrendered that Christ manifests Himself in His glory within us (2 Cor 3:18; Lk 14: 25-27, 33). So, taking up the Cross means after denying the self-life, allowing Jesus to live in us for the service of mankind no matter what comes on the way (Mt 10 : 16-22).

(iii) The crucified disciple is filled by the spirit of Christ after being broken and emptied. While fulfilling the plan and will of God for redemption of the fallen mankind (Gen. 3:15; Ps 40:6-8; Heb 10:5-9) Jesus the

Sadguru had to break himself from his heavenly abode (Jn 1:1, 3; Jn 17:5, 24) and come down to earth (Jn 1: 14; 6:33, 38) where he emptied himself to zero (Phil 2: 5-9) so that he was fully filled and led by the Spirit of God the father (Jn 5:17, 19-20; 6:38; 7:16). Let us look at some of the remarkable statements that Jesus made, which clearly show how emptied of self He was: Jn 5:19; 5:30; 8:28; 12:49; 14:10, etc. All his activities were of God the father who had sent him.

In the same way, the disciple accepting his Guru's call and will for a crucified life (Mt 10:37-39) needs to be broken and emptied of his self-life so that he might be filled and led by the Spirit and life of Jesus. The emptied person can be filled in accordance with the capacity of the emptiness made; in other words, the more the emptiness, the more the filling of the Sprit and life of Christ. By this fellowship they (Guru and Shishya) become one in spirit (1 Cor 6:17).

(iv) Taking up the Cross means to sacrifice or crucify our sinful nature with its passions and desires (Gal 5:24)

It is because, before his fall, man was in the image and likeness of God (being spiritual, pure and powerful (Gen 1:26-28), but after his fall (Gen 3:1-24), he became sinful in nature. Since then man's sinful nature (inherited from Adam) desires what is contrary to the Spirit (God), and the Spirit what is contrary to the sinful nature or self-life (Gal 5:17). Man in sinful nature is a slave to the law of sin (Rom 7:25). The natural man has a desire to do good but due to his sinful nature what he wants to do he cannot do and the evil which he hates, he does it (Rom 7:15, 19). Therefore, the true disciples (or saints, or devotees) who belong to Jesus crucify (Sacrifice) their sinful nature with its passions and desires (Gal 5:24).

The Cross is a confluence where the sinful nature of man and the divine nature of Christ meet. Thereafter the sinful nature of the believer is washed away by the holy blood of Jesus and it is remembered no more, but the divine or spirit-filled nature goes forth.

(v) Taking up the Cross is taking shelter under the founder of sacrifice (Jesus the Sadguru), which is to receive the Spirit of Sacrificial life (Jn 1:29).

When we take shelter under Jesus, our old nature (old self) is crucified (put to death) with Jesus and we no longer live, but Christ lives in us (Rom 6:6; Gal 2:20). And we put on new self, which is being renewed in knowledge in the image of its creator (Col 3:10). This new self is controlled by the Spirit of Christ which lives in us (Rom 8:9).

(vi) Taking up the Cross is accepting Jesus as the Lamb of God slain before the foundation of the World (*Aadi Yajna*) and becoming co-workers with God.

According to Acharya James Dayal, seekers believing in *Aadi Yajna* (आदि-यज्ञ) (Rev. 13:8 ; 1 Pet 1:19 ; Jn 1:29, etc.) are co-workers with God (1 Cor 3:9). This co-operation is the daily experience in the life of devotees; they carry in their body the death of Jesus so that the life of Jesus may also be revealed in their body (2 Cor 4:10-11; Phil 2:12-13). Therefore, St. Paul says, "...our competence is from God (2 Cor 3:5). Such a new life is known as *crucified life* (क्रूस-युक्त जीवन).

(vii) All the righteous acts of an un-crucified man are like filthy rags (Isa 64:6).

St. Paul says, "Nothing good lives in him, that is, in man's sinful nature. For I have the desire to do what is good, but I cannot carry it out. For what I do is not the good I want to do; no, the evil I do not want to do–this

I keep on doing. Now if I do what I do not want to do, it is no longer I who do it, but it is the sin living in me that does it" (Rom 7: 18-20). For the sinful nature desires what is contrary to the Spirit, and the Spirit what is contrary to the sinful nature. They are in conflict with each other, so you do not do what you want (Gal 5:17).

But if you are led by the Spirit, you are not under law (Gal 5:18). St. Paul says, "Live by the Spirit, and you will not allow the desires of the sinful nature or flesh (Gal 5:16; Rom 8:9). So, self-life must be crucified before there can be any service that pleases God (Rom 12: 1-2; Eph 1:10).

(viii) The pathway to the Cross is like a grain of wheat sown in the ground.

The grain of wheat when sown in the ground undergoes many changes–it loses its lustre, withers, disfigures and dies, but is eventually transformed into new life (new plant), full of life and attraction, bearing fruit (many grains). Such was the earthly life of Jesus. It was transformed beautifully and became the source of new life for all believing mankind. So should be the life-process of a disciple.

(ix) The crucified life unites with Jesus' yoke in order to become a servant of others.

The goal of a disciple (to have a crucified life) is to take up with love and respect the yoke of the Lord upon himself (Mt 11:29) and likewise to become a servant of others (Phil 2:7-8). In this service, accepting and bearing all sorts of troubles, persecution, abuses, etc., he should go on experiencing the Cross of the Lord (Phil 3:10). On one hand, the disciple is ready to suffer persecution and all the situation against him (2 Cor 10:5), and on the other hand, through the crucified life, he goes on making progress in the knowledge of the will of God. He is able to find out what pleases the Lord (Eph 5:10).

So, he surrenders his will under the will of God the Father. The knowledge of God's will is the knowledge of His love (1 Jn 4:8, 16); therefore, the disciple's life is filled progressively in the love of God, which surpasses all knowledge (Eph 3:19). This is the goal of a Christian disciple.

He who unites himself with the Lord is one with Him in Spirit (1 Cor 6:17). He becomes the Lord's tool and led by the Spirit (Gal 5:18; Acts 11:17) and he is made new in the attitude of his mind and he puts on new self, created to be like God in true righteousness and holiness (Eph 4:25; Rom 12:1-2; 2 Cor 4:10).

(x) The Cross is a symbol of Divine Love

God's hidden love for man is manifested in His dying on a cross for man (Acts 20: 28). God the Father loved God the Son (Jesus) before the world was made (Jn 17:5, 24). This love characterises the Spirit-filled (crucified) men as well (1 Jn 3:16)–the early apostolic church took up their cross considering it the way of the divine love; the true disciples manifested the love of the Cross by actually laying down their lives for the sake of their brethren (Jn 3:16; 1 Jn 3:16) while preaching and teaching others about the Good News of Salvation in Jesus Christ.

Between the Spirit-filled (crucified) man and every other person, there is a cross on which he dies to himself in order to love the other. This is the true meaning of love. Who shall separate us from the love of Christ? Shall tribulation, or distress, or persecution, or famine, or nakedness, or peril, or sword? As it is written, for thy sake we are killed all the day long; we are accounted as sheep for the slaughter. Nay, in all these things we are more than conquerors through him that loved us. For I am persuaded, that neither death, nor life, nor angels, nor principalities, nor powers, nor things present, nor things to come, nor height, nor depth, nor any other creature, shall be able to separate us from the love of God, which is in Christ Jesus our Lord (Rom 8:35-39).

(3) Following Jesus the Sadguru

It is to be with the Guru to fulfill the purpose of God (Jn 6:39). It is obeying the Guru as did the first disciples when they left everything and followed Him (Lk 5:10-11). It is to be with Jesus to bring much fruit (Jn 15:16). It is to follow Jesus' commands, His ways, His teachings, His life style, etc., as His life was the true light of men (Jn 1:4). It is to follow Him from His Cross to heaven (the destination).

His private personal life and public social life provided the curriculum for the disciples. The life of the disciples should, therefore, be a reflection of the life of their Master.

Jesus' lifestyle must be known and all attempts must be made to follow His ways according to His wish.

Jesus had no self-desire, pride or passion. He was a great *Vairagi* as He had nothing of His own (Lk 9:58). The Guru was *Karma-yogi* (desireless of fruit or reward); He went on doing good by offering a selfless service for the helpless).

Jesus is the source of prayer for His followers. "Early in the morning while it was still dark, He used to go to a lonely place and resorted to prayer" (Mk 1:35). Prayer was His life; prayer was the inseparable union and communion between Him and His heavenly Father in carrying out all His activities for the service of mankind. That is why He could say, "I and Father are one" (Jn 10:30). Jesus is the source and teacher of Prayer. Disciples must have a life of prayer as taught by Him in Mathew 6:5-14. The prayer He taught to His disciples, known as the *Lord's Prayer* (Mt 6:9-13), is to be analysed, meditated upon and then followed and practised meaningly in daily life (which is generally not done).

As we are at the *end of the age* now, those who are watchful and pray always will be able to reach the shore. The Guru tells us all to watch for His coming. "...Take heed to yourself, lest your hearts be weighed down with carousing (dissipation), drunkenness, and cares of this life, and that Day (The Rapture as well as the Day of the Lord) come on you unexpectedly. For it will come as a snare on all those who dwell on the face of the whole earth. *Watch therefore, and pray always* that you may be counted worthy to escape all these things that will come to pass, and to stand before the Son of Man" (Lk 21:34-36; Mt 24:36-44; Mk 13:32-37).

The disciples have to follow the Guru while discharging their duties for the Mission of the Lord (Eph 2:10), as He instructed His 12 Apostles (Mt 10:5-31) and later 70 other disciples (Lk 10:1-11) when He sent them out for limited ministry. The Guru tells them to rely on God for all the material needs (Mt 6:24-30).

Discipleship is following but not looking back
Jesus asked many to follow Him (Lk 9:59-62). One replied, "Lord, first let me go and bury my father." Jesus said, "Let the dead bury their own dead, but you go and proclaim the kingdom of God."

Another replied, "I will follow you, Lord, but first let me go back and say goodbye to my family."

Jesus said, "No one who puts his hand to the plough and looks back is fit for the service in the kingdom of God" (Lk 9:59-62).

Discipleship is obeying and following the Great Commission (Mt 28:18-20; Jn 20:19-23; Acts 1:6-8 Cf; Lk 23:36-49; Jer 1:7-10)

"Go therefore and make disciples of all nations, baptising them in the name of the Father and of the Son and of the Holy Spirit" (Matt 28:19).

These words of Jesus are known as the "Great Commission." These words are His final `marching orders' to the eleven disciples who had been His companions for three years. These disciples were now commanded to bring the message of new life to the whole world. And we know that by the power and grace of the Holy Spirit upon them, they were able to carry out this commission.

But these words of Jesus were not applicable to only those eleven disciples. This great commission was taken seriously by others as well, and as a result, Christianity flourished throughout the world. We, too, have been commissioned by Jesus to "make disciples of all nations."

This commission may appear to us as something very difficult and we may shrink back from it. But we should never forget that Jesus Himself ended His commission with the comforting words: "I am with you always, to the close of the age" (Mt 28:20). We can stand on this promise. He will be with us as we carry out his commission, which is to go on till the close of the age. He will help us to overcome fear, pride, or anything else that deters us from preaching His word.

The Great Commission involves four things

(i) Preparation for the Commission (Acts 1:8; Jer 1:7-10)

(ii) Going and teaching all nations. Unless a person knows his bondage in sin, he will not seek release; unless he knows that Christ is the sin-bearer of the world, he will not think of Him. So, teaching is to bring people *to faith* in Jesus Christ's redemptive work, a requirement to be counted righteous before God (Rom 1:17; 5:1 ; 9:30; 10:4) and a requirement to receive the saving grace of God (Eph 2:8).

While teaching people of other nations, their cultural background should be understood, respected and taken into consideration. Our teaching method should be guided by the Teacher–the Holy Spirit.

(iii) Baptising the believing people in the name of Triune God. The believing persons are to be baptised in the name of Triune God (Father, the Son and the Holy Spirit). This permission with authority is the Sacrament or *Deeksha Samskara* granted by Jesus the Sadguru. Jesus commands His disciples to repeat and convey His commands to other people of the world and impart the *Deeksha Samskara*. This sacrament is the baptism of Divine Knowledge (*para jnana*).

This *Deeksha Samskara* (sacrament) takes the disciple to a group of "new-born people" or "born-again people" for such people are said to have been born from above (to be Children of God). Of course, these blessings are received by faith only (Acts 8:35-39). This birth from God is called new birth (Jn 3:3, 5, 7). New birth is spirit-filled life. This birth, given by the Guru, is also called *Brahma-Janma*. It is superior to natural birth.

So, sacrament in the name of Triune God unites every disciple with God, which is the ultimate purpose of life in the sight of Jesus the Sadguru.

(iv) The disciples have to make disciples. The Great Commission is for disciples to make disciples and teach them all the things they have already been taught by their Guru. It involves leading them to perfect life by teaching, preaching, healing, performing miracles and making them aware of God's plan to be in union with Him by living like Jesus the Sadguru and depending much on the utility and exercise of the spiritual gifts of the disciples who make other disciples.

Through *baptism* (sacrament or *Deeksha Samskara* of the Guru), Jesus lives in us. He who died for us and rose again has given *new life* to His disciples; the disciples can rejoice now and in heaven—when they share that life with others. There are many ways of sharing our new life with others— we can feed the hungry, comfort the lonely, visit the sick; we can work to correct injustice in our society; we can work as peacemakers in disturbed homes and communities; we can show God's presence with us by loving one another (Jn 13 : 34-35; Mat 5:43-48); we can show the standard of life by living the life taught by Jesus in Sermon on the Mount (Mt chapters 5, 6 and 7). The force of new life will help us in winning people as required by the Great Commission (Mt 28:19).

Finally, our new life *in* Christ and Christ's life *in* us should be seen by others to be united with our Creator, who created us in Christ Jesus for good works (Eph 2:10). In doing all such things, we establish God's kingdom on earth.

The Apostles and later other disciples carried out the Great Commission to spread the Gospel. May God give His grace to us all who can continue to carry out His Great Commission with courage, knowing that He will be with us always (Mt 28:20)

For Christ's followers (Jn 21:17), following is also caring (feeding).

Jesus charged His disciple Peter to 'Feed His sheep' or to take care of His followers (Jn 21:15-19). What did Jesus see in Peter that he entrusted the future life and ministry of His Church to him? It was not Peter's wisdom that enabled him to care for Christ's followers, it was not pastoral gifts (though these gifts can be important), or Peter's leadership qualities that prompted Jesus to say, "Feed my sheep." The single quality that enabled Peter to care for Christ's' followers was his love for Jesus: "Lord, you know that I love You" (Jn 21:16; cf 13:37; Mt 26:33; Mk 14:29). Andrew Murray, a pastor and prolific writer in South Africa during the nineteenth century, pondered on the meaning of three words: *Feed my sheep*. The following is a summary of his insights:

To *feed* is to give to others what will help them grow. Every Christian must consider how to help others to grow: How can we explain Jesus' words so that they understand? How can we nurture a desire in them to turn to God?

The word *my* means that these sheep belong to Jesus. The work we do in caring for the Master's sheep involves hard work and initiative. But we must always remember that we nurture them for the Lord, not for the fulfillment of our own wishes or desires. They belong to Him.

And what are sheep? Sheep depend upon their shepherds to create an environment that is safe, healthy and good for their growth. A precious lot are weak and in constant need of care. In a similar way, all Christians are in one way or another sheep in need of care. We have a responsibility to care for them and feed them with the food Jesus gives. (*Meditations on the Gospel According to St John* by Fr Joseph A. Mindling, O.F.M. Cap pp 197-198).

Following is practising Jesus' New Commandment of Love.

Disciples need to love one another as Jesus had loved His disciples. Jesus said, "A new commandment I give unto you, that you love one another; as I have loved you, that you also love one another. By this all men will know that you are My disciples, if you have love for one another." (Jn 13:34-35).

Jesus said, "Love one another, as completely as He loves us." Jesus loves us with a love that gives everything, and possesses and keeps nothing for itself. The Father and the Son are one in that love. All that the Father is and has, He has given to Jesus. As with the Father, Jesus gave Himself totally for the sake of love (Jn 10:11; 15:13). He did not consider even His life or His body too much to give for us.

As we accept the love that Jesus had for us, we are empowered to give the same love freely to others. As we give away the love that we have received, we become co-worker with the God, whose mission is to draw the entire world to Jesus (Mt 28: 19-20). Through our share in divine love, God's everlasting life can be magnified and good news of salvation can go forth.

Undoubtedly, love has the power to change the world, the love of God is poured into human hearts by the Holy Spirit (Gal 5:22-23). It is the love of God that flows between His people as they lay down their lives for one another. We can come to know the love of God by praying, by reading the Scriptures, by receiving Jesus in Holy Communion and by obeying God's commandments. Divine love makes people fearless (1 Jn 4:18), creates God-consciousness and Christ-consciousness, inspires them to deal with the world with divine love and makes their life right with their Creator, Redeemer and Sustainer.

The Bible says,

> Whoever loves his brother lives in the light, and so there is nothing in him that will cause someone to sin. But whoever hates his brother is in the darkness, he walks in it and does not know where he is going, because the darkness has made him blind (1 Jn 2:10-11).

> Whoever does not love is still under the power of death. Whoever hates his brother is a murderer, and you know that a murderer has not got eternal life in him (1 Jn 3:14-15).

> This is how we know what love is: Christ gave His life for us. We too, then, ought to give our lives for our brothers...Our love should not be just words and talk; it must be true love, which shows itself in action (1 Jn 3:16-18).

> God is love" (1 Jn 4:8). "He loved us and sent His Son to be the means by which our sins are forgiven....No one has ever seen God, but if we love one another, God lives in union with us, and His love is made perfect in us (1 Jn 4 :10-12).

All disciples must follow the Sermon on the Mount (Mt 5-7). The Sermon on the Mount (Mt chapters 5-7 and Luke 6:17-49) is a character sketch of those who have already entered the Kingdom and a description of the quality of ethical life that should be the standard of life for all Christians.

Both Mathew and Luke place the Sermon in the first year of Jesus' public ministry (just after a few months of His Galilean ministry spent in Synagogue preaching). The Sermon is addressed primarily to disciples (Mt 5: 1, 2; Lk 6:20). It may also be for those who had deserted paganism for life in the kingdom (Mt 5:13). Yet at the close of each account (Mt 7:28-29; Lk 7:1), we note the presence of others.

An Analysis of the Sermon

(a) The blessedness of those in the kingdom (Mt 5:3-16). The Beatitudes (5:3-10) and role of disciples in an unbelieving world (5:11-16).

(b) Fulfilment and Reformation — the relationship of Jesus to the old order (Mt 5:17-18) (i) Jesus fulfills the law and prophets but does not condemn them (5:17); (ii) Jesus enlarges the theme, (thesis) of the law (5:18-20): He is not speaking against observing all the requirements of the law, but against hypocritical, pharisaical legalism (*Karma Kand*). Jesus refuses to acknowledge the interpretation of the Law by the Pharisees and their view of righteousness by works. He preaches a righteousness that comes only through faith in Him and His work. (iii) The Theme or Reformation is illustrated (5:21-48): Here the six areas of life (murder, adultery, divorce, oaths, retaliation (revenge) and hatred) have to be changed, reformed or transformed into victory by being in Lord Jesus Christ (Jn 15:5). Jesus as a New Moses asks His disciples to overcome all the six areas in order to have a perfect or complete life (5:48).

In overcoming the six areas of life, *anger* has to be rooted out as it leads to murder (5:21-26); a lustful heart nourishing on impure desires has to be changed in order to get rid of *adultery; divorce* should not find any way except adultery; kingdom righteousness demands transparent honesty, so *oaths* are unnecessary; overcome evil by good–*retaliation* will find no way.

Love is universal in application. All must be loved including the enemies by the disciples of Jesus the Sadguru, behaving as Sons of God (5:43-47). The Sadguru wants His disciples to be as perfect as the heavenly Father (5:48). Christ sets up a high ideal of perfect love (5:43-47). The disciples must look for that perfection of God in their lives (5:48).

(c) Practical instructions for the kingdom conduct (Mt 6: 1-7:12):

(i) Guard against false piety (6:1-18) in almsgiving (6:1-4), in prayer (6:5-15) and in fasting (6:16-18).

(ii) Dispel anxiety with simple trust (6:19-34) by seeking first the kingdom of God (Rom 14:17; Mt 5:3-10) and His righteousness so that all the necessities of life may be added to us (6:33). The desires of this world called *Maya* or illusion are attractive, alluring, deceiving, entrapping and sinful. These desires of the flesh keep us away from God and His ways. When the grace of the Sadguru dispels *Maya* from the life of saints, *Maya* or illusion (desires of the world) follows the saints as their servant.

(iii) Live in love (Mt 7:1-12): The Sadguru gives a Golden Rule to us saying, "Whatever you want men to do to you, do also to them, for this is the law and the prophets" (Mt 7 : 12; Lk 6:31). This Golden Rule is found in a negative form in Rabbinic Judaism and in many other religions. It also occurs in various forms in Greek and Roman ethical teachings.

(d) Challenge to dedicated living (7:13-29):

(i) The way (to life) is narrow (7:13-14)

(ii) A good tree bears good fruit (7:15-20)

(iii) The Kingdom is for those *who hear and do* (7:21-27)

Each Christian *must* read, meditate upon and follow the Sermon on the Mount as it is the way of living taught by Jesus the Sadguru (the giver of life and light [Jn 1:4]), which will prepare in us heaven or the Kingdom of God right in this world (if followed sincerely). And if ignored, or followed according to the Old Testament view (ignoring the fulfillment and the reformations therein), the kingdom of God will be missed forever. All of us must know that our earthly life's perfection (Mt 5:48; 6:33) will be evaluated before the judgment throne or seat of the King of kings (Jesus) on the Day of Judgment. So, let us listen to this Sermon very carefully in order to practise it. In addition, the way of kingdom should be recognised as the way of the Cross (Mt 7:13-14).

CHAPTER 9

Christian Mystical Yogic Experiences

The mystics claim to have a direct consciousness of God's presence and an intuition freely given by God, which cannot be expressed in words. Mysticism is not a theology or teaching about God, but an experience of God Himself, an experience that stills the troubled heart, fills the heart with peace, joy and love and greatly promotes spiritual progress. Mysticism springs from an intense devotional life and enriches the devotional life.

Most mystics undergo what they call 'the dark night of the soul,' a period when there is some sort of despair, blankness, terrible experience of one's unworthiness and so on. They believe this is necessary to purify and draw out the pure love of God, which is the characteristic of a true mystic.

There were many mystics in the seventeenth century in France. They were full of heavenly light and vision, living holy and devoted lives; many of them women; many humble and ignorant; and some of them were highly educated and able Church leaders. It was through these mystics that a light shone in the Gallican Church of the seventeenth century. This mystic movement in France was imported from Spain where the leading mystic was St. Teresa of Avila (1515-1583), who caused a great reform among the Carmelites, and from Italy where the leading mystic was Philip Neri (1513-1595), who solved the problems of having discipline without rules.

Madame Acarie is regarded as the greatest and the most influential French mystic. It was she who did the most to purify the convent life of women in France. Her greatest contribution was the reform of the religious sisterhood in France. She founded the Carmelites, with the help of Teresa's sisters, who came from Spain, and later she herself joined it after her husband's death in 1613. Many of the ladies she trained became instruments for the reformation of nunneries in France. One of her daughters also became a nun.

She started receiving her mystic experiences after six years of married life, when she was twenty-two years old. Her mystic experiences were often accompanied by painful and prolonged bodily convulsions, but in her later years she could control these convulsions. It is said that she found the stigmata (scars) of the Lord like Francis of Assisi in her body.

Her mystical experience gave her great wisdom in dealing with problems and circumstances, guiding and directing her to help souls in trouble and to discern spirits.

She had no room for selfishness, as her heart brimmed over with immense love for God and mankind, which motivated many to follow the path of holiness.

St. Theresa of Spain said that in a few moments of mystic experience, "We receive without words more light than we could acquire in many years by all our terrestrial industry (worldly labour)." This inward experience of God is often accompanied by outward manifestations like falling into an ecstatic trance, becoming unconscious, seeing visions, hearing voices, etc. But these are not proofs of mysticism. They are the price that weak people have to pay in order to receive the intuition.

Mystics such as Francis de Salvs (1567-1622), Jean de Chantal (1572-1641) Piere de Berulle (1575-1629) Vincent de Paul (1576-1660), Madame Guyon (1648-1717) and Fenelon (1651-1715) are known for their good work and radiant lives.

Christian mysticism can also be observed and learnt in Christ's teaching about prayer in Matthew 6:5-14. It involves going to a room, closing the door—only to be seen by the Heavenly Father—and praying to the heavenly Father, who sees in secret and rewards the praying person. In this silence and solitude, the praying person comes in close contact or direct contact with his Creator and is aware of oneness with Him. The presence of God *sees all, observes all and records all.* We must recognise the presence of God (Mt 6:5; Jn 14:23) and be united with Him in Spirit (Jn 15:5; 1Cor 6:17).

Before Jesus started His ministry, the praying persons knew God as the all-knowing, all-powerful and all-caring Creator, who had delivered them from slavery, given them a homeland and fulfiled their needs. They also feared Him and trembled at His name–so sacred was His name that they dared not even pronounce it, but used other words.

Then came Jesus. When His disciples asked Him to teach them how to pray, He told them to address God as "Abba, meaning "Dad." He was telling them that as a result of His incarnation and forthcoming death and resurrection, they would be able to relate to God in a totally new way–as God's loving and beloved children.

The Lord's Prayer is based on this intimate relationship with God. He is our Father because we have become His children through the blood of Jesus. Because the Holy Spirit dwells in us we are brought to spiritual life in God. We share in the very holiness of Jesus, and so we can say with Him "Abba." It is only when our hearts know God in this way we can bless His name and long for the coming of His kingdom and doing His will on earth as it is in heaven; and can ask Him to provide for our daily needs, to deliver us from the evil one.

Prayer is sitting humbly and quietly at God's feet and listening to the still, small voice of our heavenly Father in our solitude, silence, meditation, contemplation, communion and prayer (as was observed in the lifestyle of Jesus). In such a situation, the Holy Spirit inspires us to be with God. He unites us with God, and the person can have a yogic and mystical experience through this union and communion in prayer.

The union and communion between man and God are further strengthened and become more pronounced when we fulfil the following three needs of God taught in the Lord's Prayer. The needs are:

(i) *Hallowing God's name.* God is holy and the Bible says He wants His people to be holy. Seraphims proclaim His holiness (Isaiah 6:2-3); four living creatures of Rev. 4:8 proclaim his holiness–day and night without ceasing; a host of angels sing His praises (Rev 5:11); Hanna declared that none is holy like the Lord God (1 Sam 2:2). God expects His people to be holy (Lev. 19:2; Lev 20:7. Mt 5:8, etc.). The ultimate aim of God is to have a nation of holy people because He is holy (Jude 14; 2 Pet 3:13). This bond of holiness between God and man is a yogic and mystical experience.

(ii) *Coming of God's Kingdom* (Mt 6:10) It is longing for God's Spirit to rule and lead our life. It is to be a new creation in Christ. It is to have life of righteousness and peace and joy in the Holy Spirit (Rom 14:17) Jesus said, "The kingdom of God is at hand." It is near, but can be had by following Jesus with a childlike heart. God's kingdom can be achieved by fighting against and resisting Satan in union with God (Ja 4:7).

(iii) *Doing of God's will on earth* (Mt 6:10). It is doing of His will in our lives by living for him, living with Him but finally living in Him; and asking Him anything according to His will, He hears and we gain more confidence in him. God is searching people who worship Him in spirit and truth and ask anything and receive anything if it is asked according to His will (1 Jn 5:14).

The study, analysis, meditation and contemplation of the above passage (Mt 6:5-14) would unite every searching and thirsty person with his Creator (God) as branches are united with vine (Jn 15:2). Mysticism is not limited to a monastic life; Christians should always live in deep awareness of their mystical union in Christ. This would bring consistency in daily walk, effectiveness and fullness of joy in the Holy Spirit. Such people will enter into mystical fulfillment and rivers of living water will flow from their innermost being, that is, heart (Jn 7: 37-38).

In his book, *Fulfilment of Vedic Quest in Lord Jesus Christ*, Acharya Daya Prakash Titus mentions *yogic* and mystical experiences. These two important experiences can be viewed as follows: The ultimate goal of soul or spirit (*jeevatma*) in both Hinduism and Christianity is its Union in the Supreme Spirit. The word *yoga* means to bind, to join, or to unite. Mysticism is a quest of the soul for union and communion with its creator–an experience of the divine life flowing into its own.

Christianity, like other religions, has a strong mystical element. Medieval Christianity inherited a continuity of mysticism but it remained the privilege of few. *Christian mysticism is a spiritual love between God and man. It is a thirst of soul for the living God as felt deeply by David* (Psalm 42:1), who was a man after God's own heart. Christ taught Christian mysticism, His mysticism was often to be observed in His solitude, silence, listening to the still voice of the Heavenly Father, meditation, contemplation, communion and prayer. His words were spirit and truth (Jn 6:63). He taught that God and man ought to be united like branches are with vine (Jn 15:2).

Christian mysticism is for all. It is obeying Christ's words, which are spirit and truth. Jesus said, "What gives life is God's Spirit; man's power is of no use at all. The words I have spoken to you bring God's life-giving spirit (Jn 6:63). He has given an invitation to all to enter into mystical fulfilment: "If any man thirsts, let him come to Me and drink. He who believes in Me, as the Scripture has said, out of his heart (innermost being) will flow rivers of living water (Jn 7:37-38). This Jesus spoke concerning the spirit.

Yoga (union of soul or spirit in the Supreme Spirit) in the Bible is not any system or discipline of experience, but rather the result of the descent of God into our life through our Lord. This union in Christ is an important doctrine of the Bible and can be seen by the frequent use of the word *IN* in a mystical way. Other words such as *As* and *with* also express union and our relationship in *yoga*. For example, "Know ye not that Christ is *in* you?" (2 Cor 13:5); "Abide *in* Me and I in you" (Jn 15:4); "Hereby we know that we live in Him and He *in* us, because He his given us His Spirit" (1 Jn 4 :13); "I have been crucified with Christ and I no longer live, but Christ lives *in* me" (Gal 2:20); "Whoever obeys God's commands lives *in union* with God and His love is made perfect in us" (1 Jn 3:24; 4:12); "If anyone declares that Jesus is the Son of God, he lives *in union* with God and God lives *in union* with him" (1 Jn 4:15); "*As* the Father has loved Me, so I have loved you. Dwell in My love" (Jn 15:9); "That all of them may be one, Father, just *as* you are in Me and I am in you" (Jn 17:21); "But you know the Spirit, for He lives *with* you, and will be *in* you" (Jn 14:17).

The union we have in Christ is complete and perfect, says the Scripture: "For in Christ all the fullness of the Godhead lives in bodily form and you have been given fullness *in union* with Him" (Col 2:9-10).

Here are some illustrations of the *type* of *union* existing between God and the believer.

(a) *As vine and its branches* (Jn 15:5)

(b) *As yoke of oxen.* "Take my yoke upon you...learn of me...find rest" (Mt 11:29). Here the new and young disciple is like a new and young ox who has to be yoked or united with his Guru, who is trained and expert. The main weight or pull will fall upon the Master.

(c) *As the temple and its stones* (Eph 2:21-22 Cf.1 Pet 2:4-5).

(d) *As husband and wife* (Eph 5:22-23).

(e) *As man and woman.* "For it is said, "The two will become one flesh. But he who unites himself with the Lord is one with Him in the Spirit" (1 Cor 6:15-17).

(f) *As the human body* in which every part is a member of the whole (Cor 12:12-13).

(g) *As the Father God and His Son.* "Father just as you are *in* Me and I am *in* you, may they also be in us, so that the world may believe that you sent Me" (Jn 17:21).

In Hinduism, the true yoga union or *milan* between God and man is a rare achievement and certainly not accessible in one lifetime. But in Christianity, the believer can achieve it right here in this one life by giving heed to the call of Jesus, "Take my yoke (*yoga*)...and you will find rest for your souls. For my yoke is easy..." (Mt. 11:29-30).

The union of soul or spirit in the Supreme Spirit has been given in *The Song of Songs* or *The Song of Solomon*. It is in the form of love poems. These songs have been interpreted by Jews as a bridal relationship between God and His people and by Christians as a picture of relationship between Christ and the Church. In 1909, an English Scholar, Dr. J. Rendel Harris, discovered nearly a complete copy of the odes of Solomon consisting of 42 odes or songs. Here is the third ode.

I should not have known how to love the Lord
    If He had not loved me
for who is able to grasp the meaning of love
    except the one that is loved?

I love the Beloved
    and my soul loves Him
and where His rest is
    there also am I
and I shall be no stranger
    for with the Lord most high and merciful
there is no keeping back.

I have been united with Him
    for the Lover has found the beloved
and because I shall love Him that is the Son
    I shall become a son
for he that is united to Him who never dies
    will also himself become immortal

and he who has pleasure in the Living One
    will become alive.
This is the Spirit of the Lord
    and does not lie
who teaches the sons of men to know His ways.
   be wise and understanding and vigilant
Hallelujah.

                  (Decision Magazine, *October 1975*)

St. Augustine reflected the immanence of God in himself: "I sought Thee at a distance, and did not know that Thou wast near. I sought Thee abroad in Thy works, and behold, Thou wast in me."

In his *Thoughts in Solitude,* Thomas Merton has offered an interesting differentiation between living *for,* living *with* and living *in* God:

(a) Those who live *for* God live with other people in the activities of their community; their life is what they do

(b) Those who live *with* God live not in what they do *for* him but in what they *are* before him; and

(c) Those who live *in* God do not live *with* other men, or in themselves; still less in what they do, for God does all things *in* them.

Pundit Narayana Vaman "Tilak," one of our own poets, has expressed his yoga experience in Christ in his work, *Bhakti Niranjana*:

    As lyre and the musician,
    As thought and spoken word,
    As rose and fragrant odours,
    As flute and breath accord;
    So deep the bond that binds me
    To Christ my Lord.

As mother and her baby,
As traveller lost and guide,
As oil and flickering lamp-flame,
Are each to each allied;
Life of my life, Christ bindeth
Me to His side.

As lake and streaming rainfall,
As fish and water clear,
As sun and gladdening dayspring
In union close appear;
So Christ and I are holden
In bonds how dear!

The diversity in *yoga* unity is explained by Tilak to be like the painter's art which combines different colours into one scene; like children in the home who are different but make one home; like the poet who uses many words and makes one lovely strain; like stars with differing glow which shed one heavenly radiance below; like divergent notes on the piano which make one harmony. "Souls that differ endlessly, to one world-Soul may welded be."

Recording her experience, the famous writer, J. Penn-Lewis writes, "He that is joined unto the Lord is One Spirit" (1 Cor. 6.17). Here is set forth clearly the union with Christ in the spirit, which is the purpose and outcome of the work of the Cross. This union with the risen and ascended Lord can be only in spirit and experimentally realised as the spirit of the believer is separated from the unwrapping of the soul... (Soul and Spirit, p 38).

Tilak writes:

Grant, Lord, the prayer that I present:
Whatever there be of self in me,

Let all be swallowed up in Thee
Two persons in one Spirit blent.

(Bhakti Niranjana 1.17)

The above are only a few samplings of the variety of Christian mysticism that has existed here and there in the body of the Church.

Christ's Disciples as Yogis

John's Gospel depicts the life of a Christian disciple as a yogi who:

- Believes in Christ (14.1)
- Is liberated from bondage (8.32)
- Is born of God (1.13)
- Has eternal life (3.16)
- Has the peace of Christ (14.27)
- Has the full joy of the Lord (15.11; 16.22-24)
- Loves the Father and the Son (14.21)
- Has friendship with Jesus (15.14-15)
- Is indwelt by the Holy Spirit (14.17)
- Is loved of the Father (16.27)
- Abides or dwells in Jesus Christ (15.4)
- Knows God the Father in Christ (14.7)
- Bears fruit for Jesus (15.5)
- Is united with God and the Son (17.11, 21-23, 26)
- Is sharing in the Mission of Christ (17.18; 15.27)
- Loves the children of God (15.17)
- Is persecuted by the world (15.20- ; 17.14-16)
- Glorifies Christ (17.10)

When a separated sinner repents and is restored by the grace of God, he has the privilege of knowing God in experience, and God can best be known in His oneness, not in the unreality of separation. *Moksha* or salvation is essentially that state of experience when duality is over and man finds the essential unity in God. Knowledge of one's own inner standing is essential. Knowing God and his Son Jesus Christ is eternal life (Jn 17:3). Unless a person knows his bondage in sin, he will not seek release.

The will of God for man is his liberation. The aim of Christianity is to abide in Christ. It is participation with Him. This Christian Yoga leads to activity in the mission of Christ according to Jn 5:17: "My Father is working still and I am working." Such activity produces fruit for the glory of God (Jn 15:8). Yoga is also a unifying factor in the life of the community (Jn 17: 23).

According to the Bible, *yoga* is not a product of our physical effort or austerity. Yoga is not the cancellation of the beautiful gift of mind given to us by God. It is not realised in attempting withdrawal of the senses but the surrender of the senses to the service of God and mankind. The Gospel promises that it is accessible. Yoga is not for a few, but for everyone, regardless of caste, creed, race or colour. It is for those who have faith, courage and determination to receive it from God.

The Spirit of the human being is thirsty for the living God (Psalm 42:1-2). It is thirsty for reunion with the source of the living water (Jn 7:37-38). The yoga of Christ, therefore, has to be taught to our generation. Any preaching of the Good News without yoga will not meet the need of the Sons of the Sages (the *rishis*). India has the thirst for that water.

According to Acharya Daya Prakash, Christian Yoga has the marks of fulfilment of all the principal yoga doctrines of the Vedanta, such as Jnana Yoga, Karma Yoga and Bhakti Yoga, as the Christian Yogi has found *gnana* (knowledge), which is Christ; he as *Karma Yogi* engages himself in the mission of love and compassion to the world, desireless of obtaining a reward; and lives a life of *bhakti*, devotion and surrender to the Lord. The *yogi* lives in the realisation that all things belong to the Lord—the whole creation and all that is in it. "And God has placed all things under the feet of Jesus and appointed Him to be Head over everything for the Church, which is His body, the fullness of Him who fills everything in every way" (Eph 1 : 22-23).

> So then no more boasting about men! All things are yours, whether Paul or Apollos or Caiphas, or the world or life or death or present or future—all are yours, and you are of Christ and Christ is of God.
>
> (1 Cor 3: 21-23)

> When to man all beings become the very Self, then what delusion and what sorrow can there be left for him?
>
> (Isha Upanishad-7)

> In that day you will know that am IN My Father and you IN Me and I IN you.
>
> (Jn 14: 20)

Prof. Friedrich Heiler views the Life of Sadhu Sundar

Sadhu Sundar Singh is regarded as part of the family of Christian mystics. Taking a look at the life of Sadhu Sundar Singh, *Prof F. Heiler* says, "In his inner life he is most closely related to the family of Christian mystics. His love of solitude, and contemplation, his steady practice of meditation and reflection, his theocentric method of prayer, his frequent visions and ecstasies, his conceptions of heaven—all these things point in the direction of mysticism.

The fact that he unites a strenuous life of work in the service of the brethren with a rich contemplative experience does not lessen his right to be called a *mystic;* indeed, it is a supreme mark of the Christian mystic to be able to combine the *contemplative life* (saintly quietness) with the *active life* (necessary activity), the *alternation of saintly quietness and necessary activity,* as Bernard of Clairvaux so beautifully puts it. But it is a striking fact that a mind like his, which has so much in common with the Christian mystics, should yet be in such close agreement with Martin Luther, who was the very opposite of a mediaeval mystic in his conception of the central doctrine of Christianity, of Christ and salvation, of faith and work.

CHAPTER 10

Price of Discipleship

The early Christians were asked to give up their discipleship of Jesus or be thrown before the hungry lions in the *arena*. Some were tied behind running chariots, while others were placed in hot oil pans. But those disciples did not count the suffering of this world any greater than the joy and glory they had received in Jesus Christ. What a price they paid!

In addition, in the same city of Rome, the disciples facing threats of death took refuge in the underground dark caves (catacomb), where no enemy would touch them. But there their families and children died one after another owing to hunger, thirst and disease. These underground caves were often used as tombs. These graves still exist in the walls. Many of theses graves are marked with four Roman letters "VITA", which means life. In the midst of death, they were able to think and write of life. This was discipleship.

St. Thomas, an apostle of the Sadguru, visited India as well (Punjab in 46 A.D. to 52 A.D. and South India in 52 A.D. to 72 A.D.). He lived a saintly life, established churches by the power of the Holy Sprit and authority and presence of his Guru. He received great honour in the south, but was martyred in Mylapur (Chennai) in 72 A.D.

Sadhu Sundar Singh, a Sikh sadhu of Punjab, surrendered his life to Lord Jesus Christ even from his early youth. He had visions of Jesus. He lived for Jesus. His life was *in* Jesus and Jesus was *in* him. He always saw God and remained with Him in his God-consciousness and Christ-consciousness. His profound preaching astonished the Christian world and many sadhus, sanyasis, and Vedantis in the Himalayan regions of India.

Sadhu Sundar Singh often used to go to Tibet to preach the good news of Jesus the Sadguru. He was often tortured there. Once he was thrown into a dark well to die. But God's providence took him out while he could see no man there.

Similarly, another Sikh youth, Sardar Kartar Singh, who also went to Tibet to spread the Good News of the Gospel, was captured, sewn into wet Yak skins and left in the sun to die. He died after the third day, but even when he was dying, his prayers, witness, and copy of the New Testament saved the life of the attending Chief Secretary of Lama. What a discipleship!

Besides, Pastor Graham Staines, a servant of God and social worker, made a great sacrifice when he and his two sons were burnt alive by some cruel people. Mrs. Staines suffered such a great tragedy in the family, but her enlightened Christ-and-Holy-Spirit-led life expressed her forgiveness to the culprits in the midst of her deep sorrow. What a costly and faithful discipleship it is!

In the history of the Christian Church, there have been many disciples who chose to pay the price of discipleship. There is no country in the world where true disciples of Jesus did not show their faithfulness even unto death. And the blood shed by the disciples of Jesus has always turned out to be the 'seed' of the church.

CHAPTER 11

Rewards of Discipleship

Let us also consider the rewards of this discipleship.

(1) **Acknowledged by Christ (Mt 12:49-50)**
And He (Jesus) stretched out His hand towards His disciples and said, "Here are My mother and My brothers. For whoever does the will of My Father in heaven is My brother and sister and mother."

(2) **Enlightened by Christ (Jn 8:12)**
"Then Jesus spoke to them again, saying, 'I am the light of the world. He who follows Me shall not walk in darkness, but have light of life.'" Guru means light, and Jesus is the light of the world; His disciples walk in that light.

(3) **Guided by the Spirit (Jn 16:13)**
"However, when He, the spirit of truth, has come, He will guide you into all truth; for the Holy Spirit will not speak on His own authority, but whatever He hears He will speak; and He will tell you things to come." (Jn 16:13 Acts11:28; Rev. 1:19).

(4) **Disciples honored by the Father: Jesus spoke to the Greeks through His disciples**
"If anyone serves Me, let him follow Me; and where I am, there My servant will be also. If any serves Me, him My Father will honour" (Jn 12:26).

Jesus said "If anyone loves Me, he will keep My word; and My Father will love him, and We will come to him and make Our home with him" (Jn 14:23; cf Mt 16:24; Jn 14:3; 17:24 etc).

(5) **Disciples Earn Privilege of God's Revelation**

(i) Sadhu Sundar Singh, a well-known Sikh Sadhu of Punjab, who had surrendered his life to Christ, had taken his cross from his very early youth and united with Christ and remained so throughout his life. Many sadhus and sanyasis of our country and abroad were highly impressed by his profound knowledge of God or Truth, which they found in his teaching and personal life. He was always God-conscious and Christ-conscious and was never without God.

Sundar Singh's needs were met by God's voluntary will. Once he lost his way in a jungle and found himself near the bank of a rivulet late in the evening, which he had to cross to be saved from wild animals and to be in a safer place in a nearby village. As he attempted to cross this fast-flowing rivulet, someone shouted and stopped him from crossing it. In order to save the sadhu, the stranger lifted him on his back and crossed the rivulet. The stranger placed the sadhu in a safer place, lit a fire and gave him some food to eat.

The stranger disappeared while Sundar Singh was eating. This stranger was none other than the angel of the Lord. What a great privilege to be a sincere disciple of Jesus the Sadguru!

Again, Sadhu Sundar Singh was thrown by the order of head Lama into a dark well in a deserted place in Tibet. But here too the Sadhu was saved by God's providence.

(ii) St. Paul also surrendered his life to Jesus the Sadguru. He says, "I have been crucified with Christ and I no longer live, but Christ lives in me" (Gal 2:20).Many a time he found himself in life-endangering situations, but death could not hold him. Lord Jesus Christ had chosen and appointed him for the great task of building churches in many countries and proclaiming salvation through Him.

St. Paul was able to establish many churches and reveal many mysteries surrounding the second coming of Jesus. He also had 'Vision of Paradise' (2 Cor 12:1-4).

The true church of Christ has the privilege to be lifted up in heaven by Jesus Himself (Jn 14:1-3; Mt 24:40-41; 1 Thess 4:16-18). What a privilege for a few to be alive in the clouds to meet the Lord! This is a great privilege for those dead in Christ, as they will be lifted up first; and the living faithful ones will be lifted up to join them in the clouds to meet the Lord. This is the greatest privilege for all those who lived in Christ and all those who continue to live in Him.

(iii) The Maharishi of Kailash enjoys the privilege of immortality; he has the privilege of living bodily till the second coming of Christ. What a wonderful privilege! This mystery was revealed by Sadhu Sundar Singh. In the summer of 1921, he went to Kailash (a holy hilltop in the Himalayan range where many Hindu sadhus and rishis reside). At Kailash, Sadhu Sundar Singh saw a cross of stone standing on a rock; he was astonished and wanted to find out the truth about it, but owing to his long and tiresome journey, he unfortunately got lost. After many days of wandering, he decided to go down the hilltop of Kailash. While going down the hill he stumbled and fell. When he came round, he found himself in front of the cave of this very old man. The body of the old man was fully covered by hairs. He had long nails and his eyebrows hung over his face. This old saint had a big leather copy of the New Testament. After reading the fifth chapter of Matthew to Sadhu Sundar Singh, he prayed on his knees and concluded his prayer in the name of Lord Jesus Christ. This old sage told Sadhu Sundar Singh that he was born 318 years ago in a Muslim family in Alexandria (Egypt) and that at the age of 30 he renounced the world and became a sanyasi and vairagi, but could not find peace. It was only after he met St. Yernaus, a Christian preacher (nephew of the world famous Francis Xavier [1506-1558]), that he found peace.

The sage embraced Christianity later and travelled around the world with St. Yernaus. Afterwards, he preached the Gospel independently for 75 years, till the age of 105 years. In this span of time, he learnt twenty languages.

When he was 105 years old he went to Kailash to constantly pray in solitude for the Gospel preachers of the world. Then he prayed to God to take him to His heavenly abode and let him rest in peace. While he was praying he heard the sound of hundreds of birds fluttering through the air in his cave, but he could see nothing. The saint knelt down and prayed and asked God to reveal the mystery and show him His will. While he was praying he felt as if someone had touched his eyes. When he opened his eyes he saw hundreds of angels in the cave. He also saw a host of angels coming down the heaven singing the glory of God. The old saint fell on his knees and praised and worshipped the Almighty God. God held his hand lovingly, lifted him up and said, "O my faithful servant! I grant you everlasting life, you will live till My second coming, which is very close. You will live to pray for the churches.

The maharishi was congratulated by the saints who had come down from heaven. Since then he met many saints. They visited him to help him with God's work. Another gift that God gave him was *that he could travel in spirit* around the world *leaving his body right in the cave.* The maharishi *could also visit heaven.*

(6) **Reward of Receiving Disciples (Mt 10:40-42)**

Jesus said, "He who receives you (disciples) receives Me, and he who receives Me receives Him who sent Me. He who receives a prophet in the name of a prophet shall receive a prophet's reward. And he who receives a righteous man in the name of a righteous man shall receive a righteous man's reward. And whoever gives one of these little ones only a cup of cold water in the name of a disciple, assuredly I say to you, he shall by no means lose his reward."

(7) **Reward of Renunciation (Mt 19:27-30; Mk 10:28-30; Luke 18:28-30)**

"Then Peter answered and said to Him (Jesus), 'See, we have left all and followed you. Therefore, what shall we have? 'So Jesus said to them,' Assuredly I say to you, that in the regeneration, when the Son of man sits on the throne of His glory, you who have followed me will also sit on twelve thrones, judging the twelve tribes of Israel. And everyone who has left houses or brothers or sisters or father or mother or wife or children or lands for my name's sake shall receive a hundred fold and inherit everlasting life. But many who are first will be last, and the last first" (Mt 19:27-30).

CHAPTER 12

True Discipleship

True Discipleship (Mt 7:21-29)

Let us now take a look at 'true discipleship' (Mt 7:21-29). "Not everyone who says to me, Lord, Lord, shall enter the kingdom of heaven, but he who does the will of My Father who is in heaven. On that day many will say to Me, Lord, Lord, did we not prophesy in Your name, and cast out demons in Your name, and do many mighty works in Your name? And then I will declare to them, I never knew you; depart from Me, you evildoers."

"Everyone then who hears these words of Mine and does them will be like a wise man who built his house upon the rock; and the rain fell, and the floods came, and the winds blew and beat upon that house, but it did not fall, because it had been founded on the rock. And everyone who hears these words of Mine and does not do them will be like a foolish man who built his house upon the sand, and the rain fell, and the floods came, and the winds blew and beat against that house, and it fell; and great was the fall of it. And when Jesus finished these sayings (the Sermon on the Mount), the crowds were astonished at His teaching, for He taught them as one who had authority, and not as their Scribes" (Matt 7:21-29).

A true disciple must be a truly spiritual person and must have an *upward look,* an *inward look* and an *outward look.* This will lead him or her to the most required practical and balanced spiritual life and the Sermon on the Mount will become the standard of his or her life.

According to Mr. Zac Poonen (Bible teacher and author of many books on deeper Christian life), a spiritual man constantly looks in three directions:

(1) *Upward*–in worship and devotion to God and Christ

(2) *Inward* – in acknowledgement and repentance of his un-Christ likeness

(3) *Outward*–in seeking to help and bless other people

The Upward Look
God has called us first of all to be his worshippers - to hunger and thirst after Him. A spiritual man worships God. His one desire is God. He does not desire anything or anyone other than God in earth or in heaven (Psa 73:25). Money does not mean more to him than God. As the deer pants for the water brooks, so the spiritual man longs for God. He longs for God more than a thirsty man longs for water. A spiritual man longs for fellowship with God more than he does for ease or comfort. He longs to hear God speak to him daily.

Those who worship money, ease or their own convenience will always find something or other to complain about. But the spiritual man never has any complaint, because he desires only God and he always has Him. He is never discouraged with the circumstances of his life, because he sees the mighty hand of God in all those circumstances and he humbles himself underneath that hand joyfully at all times.

Because a spiritual man is in touch with God, he does not need any law or rule to regulate his life. He has found the *tree of life* (God himself) and so he has no interest in the tree of knowledge of good and evil. *Because he is taken up with simple and pure devotion to Christ, he is not sidetracked by secondary issues.* Looking at Jesus, the spiritual man becomes increasingly like his Lord year by year."

The Inward Look

The upward look leads on to an inward look. As soon as Isaiah saw the glory of God, he became aware of his own sinfulness (Isa 6:1-5). It was the same with Job, Peter and John (Job 42:5, 6; Lk 5:8, Rev. 1:17). When we live in God's presence, we become aware of many areas of *un-Christ-likeness* in our lives. The spiritual man is thus constantly getting light over the hidden sins of his life.

We are commanded to worship the Lord "in holy array (dress)" (Psa 29:2). Without the clothing of holiness, we are naked before the Lord. So the spiritual man "does his best" at all times to keep his conscience clear before God and before men (Acts 24:16)... A spiritual man judges himself constantly, because he discovers many things in his life that need to be cleansed away...A spiritual man realises that he has to die inwardly every day to many things that hinder him from being effective for God...

The spiritual man has no problems in humbling himself before anyone or in asking for forgiveness from anyone...he realises that his prayers and his service will never be accepted by God, if he has hurt one other person" (Matt 5:23-24).

The Outward Look

"The upward look and inward look lead on to the outward look. A spiritual man is one who realises that God has blessed him only in order that he might be a blessing to others. Since God has forgiven him so much, he gladly and readily forgives all who have harmed him. Since God has been so good to him, he is good to others too. He has received freely from God and he gives freely to others.

A spiritual man has a keen interest in the welfare of others. He is filled with compassion for lost and suffering humanity and can never ignore a brother whom he sees in need (Lk 10:30-37).

God has great concern for the fallen man. He wants to help him, to bless him, to lift him up and to deliver him from Satan's bondage. The spiritual man's concern is the same. Like Him the spiritual man seeks to serve others and not to be served. Jesus went around delivering people who were bound by Satan (Acts 10:38). The spiritual man does the same.

A spiritual man does not seek to gain anything from others through his service for them—neither money nor honour. Like God, he only seeks to bless others through his life and work. He never expects any gifts from anyone, for he trusts in God alone for his every need...."

A spiritual man looks upward, inward and outward. If he looked only upward, he would be unrealistic —"so heavenly minded as to be of no earthly use." If he looked only inward, he would be depressed and discouraged most of the time. If he looked only outward, his work would be shallow. But a spiritual man constantly looks in all the three directions. May God help us to be balanced and spiritual (Zac Poonen, "Light of Life" The magazine for Christian Growth, October 2003, pp 27-29).

True discipleship of Jesus the Sadguru demands a spiritual life that constantly looks upward, inward and outward. Such a spiritual life is the *true way to enter into the kingdom of God* through the narrow gate as taught by Jesus the Sadguru Himself: "Enter through the narrow gate. For wide is the gate and broad is the road that leads to destruction, and many enter through it. But small is the gate and narrow the road that leads to life, and only a few find it" (Mt 7:13-14).

All the people of the world calling themselves Christians or follower of Jesus or His secret disciples must remember, review and concentrate on the words of Jesus and meditate upon them:

> For many are called (or invited), but few are chosen.
> (Mt 22:14)

> So the last will be first, and the first last. For many are called, but few chosen.
> (Mt 20:16)

> And indeed there are last who will be first, and there are first who will be last.
> (Lk 13:30)

> But many who are first, will be last and the last first.
> (Mk 10:31 -*Eternal Reward* Cf.; Mt 19:27-30; Lk 18:28-30 -*The Apostles' Reward*)

All the people calling Jesus 'Lord, Lord, shall not enter into the kingdom of heaven, unless they do the will of God the Father in heaven (Mt 7:21). The called ones should not be mistaken for inheriting the kingdom of heaven if they are not doing the will of God the Father, as it is not their birthright even to enter into the kingdom of heaven by just being born in a Christian family and not hearing and acting upon the word of God the Father and God the son and God the Holy Spirit. Jesus the Sadguru said, "And I say to you that many will come from east and west, and sit down with Abraham, Issac and Jacob in the kingdom of heaven. But the sons of kingdom will be cast into outer darkness. There will be weeping and gnashing of teeth (Mt 8:11-12 - *Seeing Great Faith of Roman Centurion)*. So, called-out people are many, but chosen are few. The living God and His Holy Spirit are always with those who are His obedient disciples (Mt 28:20).

Let all the followers of God come closer to Jesus the Sadguru to find rest (Mt 11:28), to take his yoke upon them, to learn from Him, to be obedient to His command and word, to be united with the Sadguru and live in Him (Mt 11:29; Jn 15:2; 1 Jn 4:12, 16), to bring a soul thirsty for the living God for mystical experience or spiritual love between God and man (Ps. 42:1; Jn 7:37-38) and to be obedient to His new commandment of love to love one another as taught by the Lord Jesus (to be known as His disciples[1 Jn 3: 16-24; Jn 13-34-35]).

May all the followers of God find ultimate reality and truth in Jesus the Sadguru and clothe themselves with the *Light of his life* as He is the Way, the Truth and the Life and no one comes to the Father except through Him (Jn 14:6).

Jesus the Sadguru is coming quickly as He has said, "And behold I am coming quickly, and My reward is with Me, to give to everyone according to his work" (Rev. 22:12).

CHAPTER 13

Crucified Lives

There are so many examples of disciples or crucified lives. These disciples crucified their self-life; they broke and emptied their self-life so much that they became one with God in spirit. So, their lives were led by the Spirit of God, not by their flesh or desires. They led Godly life and walked in the light of Christ.

Let us consider some examples of crucified lives to get an insight into "crucified life" or the "way of the Cross."

Abraham

He had unlimited obedience and endless willingness to sacrifice all for God. How difficult it must have been for Abraham to face the thought of sacrificing (slaying) his own son himself! "Abraham believed God, and it was credited to him as righteousness, and he was called God's friend" (Jam 2: 23). This obedience resulted in great blessings (Gen 12: 2; Gal 3:14).

The Cross of St. Paul

Apostle Paul went out to serve God and endured hardship. He received 195 stripes on his back. He was stoned and suffered shipwreck; he faced many dangers in his service to God. He endured all that because while giving his life to

Jesus, *he had determined that he would never offer to Him any service that cost him nothing.*

Paul was a love-slave of Lord Jesus: (like the Hebrew slave, Exo 21:1-6). Being a slave, he had no freedom of his own; he could be called day and night by his Master. He was not a servant (to claim wages, freedom, etc.) but he was bought by the priceless blood of his Master, so he is now a slave. The Master can take him wherever He likes; Paul just obeys; he trusts his Master. This is what is meant by "love-slave" (cf Rom 8:35-39).

God is looking for those who are committed (yielded) to Him like Paul: The Bible says, "The most important thing about a servant is that he does what his master tells him to" (1 Cor 4:2). "I sought for a man," the Lord once said, "but I found none" (Eze 22:30 cf Ps 53:2-3; 33:13; Rom 3:10-18; Ps 14:1-3). He is looking for *love-slaves* today. But He finds only a few (cf Ps. 53:2).

Paul's spirit-filled (crucified life) service recognises its debt to others: Paul said, "I am debtor to the Greeks (civilised) and to the Barbarians (un-civilised)" (Rom 1:14). God has given us a treasure to share with the World. When God entrusted him with the message of the Gospel (the message of Salvation), Paul recognised this debt to others and was always ready to go and discharge that debt. Spirit-filled service has an evangelistic passion and is perpetually outgoing.

The Cross was a symbol of weakness, shame and death. The apostle Paul had fears, perplexities, sorrows and tears in his life (See 2 Cor 1:8; 4:8; 6:10; 7:5). He was considered a fool and a fanatic. He was often treated like dirt and garbage by others (1 Cor 4:13). The sprit-filled man will find God leading him farther and farther, down the pathway of humiliation and death to Himself.

The spirit-filled man (the crucified life) does not care for the honour of men: He accepts humiliation and reproach gladly. He glories in nothing but the Cross (Gal 6:14). He does not glory in his gifts and abilities, nor even in his deeper life-experiences. He glories only in the dying to himself (Gal 2:20; 5:24).

Paul's spirit-filled life was continuously seeking greater degrees of fullness: Towards the end of his life Paul says, "I am pressing on" or "I run straight towards the goal" (Phil 3:14). He is seeking a still greater degree of fullness of the spirit of God in his life. He further says, "I am not perfect" (Phil 3:12, 15).

The spirit-filled state is not a static one: There are greater and greater degrees of fullness. The Bible says that the Holy Spirit leads us from one degree of glory to another (2 Cor 3:18), or in other words, from one degree of fullness to another. So, there will be a vast difference between the fullness of the newborn convert and fullness of a mature Apostle (like Paul). The former is like a full cup whereas the latter is like a full river (as compared by Zac Poonen). For this reason, Paul exhorts Ephesian Christians saying, "Be filled with the spirit" (Eph 5:18).

Let us take a look at Paul's exhortation about the Cross and gifts. Paul always accepted the Cross. In 2 Cor 4:10, he says, "We always carry around in our body the death of Jesus (Rom 6:6) so that the life of Jesus may also be revealed in our body" (Rom 6:5). Crucified life is a spirit-filed life (Gal 2:20). The Cross leads to the spirit and the spirit leads back to the Cross. The spirit and the Cross are inseparable (as the Cross is also a symbol of Divine love [Acts 20:28]). The Holy Spirit is constantly seeking to enlarge our capacity (Eph 5:18). There can be no enlargement in our lives if we avoid the pathway of the Cross. That is why Corinthian Christians were so shallow; they glorified in gifts and ignored the Cross. So Paul exhorts them again and again in his two epistles (Corin I & II) to accept the Cross. He exhorts them to be thereby enlarged (2 Cor 6:13). A crucified life manifests the attributes of servants of God as mentioned in 2 Cor 6:3-10.

Martin Luther

Martin Luther was born on November 10, 1483, at Eisleban. His father was a miner in Mansfield where he attended school till the age of 14.

In his disciplined home, he was taught the creed, the Ten Commandments, the Lord's Prayer and some simple hymns. Discipline was severe even at school, and religion was compulsory.

The severe discipline at school and home, and the strict catholic religion gave him the feeling of religious uncertainty and fear. God was not presented to him as a loving Father, but as a terrifying, un-approachable Being; Christ was not a merciful saviour, but a threatening and severe judge. Salvation was to be gained through mediation of saints and of the Church and by good works.

From 1498 to 1501 he was enrolled at a school (St. George Eisencah) where he had to earn his living by singing in the school choir and in the streets. He stayed in a home (of Frau Cotta) where he learned culture and refined manners; he gained many friends and a full knowledge of Latin.

In 1502 and 1505, he received his B.A. and M.A. degrees from the most celebrated Erfurt University. He was admired by all for his extra-ordinary talents. Students referred to him as the learned philosopher and musician.

In his university days, he was a good, pious Catholic; he used to perform many religious acts. But none of these produced satisfaction in him. He had no peace.

In 1505, he studied law at Erfurt. There his religious quest and search for peace increased. The same year he joined the Augustinian Monastery at Erfurt. He became a monk. He spent three years there before he saw the first ray of light and the dawn of a new day.

Let us take a look at Luther's religious struggle in the monastery.A Luther's Religious struggle in the Monastery is outlined below :

(i)   His aim was to gain divine approval and to please God.

(ii) For him sin was lack of love for God and men.

(iii) For him, the theology of Occam "Do good and after that God will give you grace" could not be fulfilled.

(iv) Another aspect of the Occam's theology "that the predestined can fulfill the requirements" terrified him, as he believed that he could not fulfil them.

(v) Dawn came through the channels: *(a)* "the words of the creed" ("I believe in the forgiveness of sins"); (b) John Staupitz's (vicar General of Germany) encouragement to read the Bible, gradually turned his attention from the works of the law to the Saviour; (c) in 1508, he began to study Augustine's teaching on sin and grace and faint rays of light began to penetrate his soul.

He began teaching in the University of Wittenberg in 1508 (where Staupitz was the Dean). In 1509, he was called to teach in the University of Erfurt. He went to Rome and remained in the city for four weeks, saw scandalous acts there and returned disappointed to Germany.

In 1512, he got his "doctor biblicus" degree. Three weeks later, he succeeded Staupitz as Professor of Theology in the University of Wittinberg, a position he held until his death in 1546.

Luther's development from 1512 to 1517

He lectured on Psalms, Romans, Galations and Hebrews. In 1512, he was appointed *sub-prior* of the Augustinian monastery at Wittinberg; he had already been appointed *preacher* in that monastery. In 1515, he was made *District Vicar* over eleven Augustinian monasteries, a position which involved a lot of correspondence and travel and by 1516 he had become so popular as a preacher that people wanted to hear him once every day. He had become equally popular as a Professor. Students from all parts of Germany came to hear him. It was probably in 1512 that he discovered the doctrine of justification by faith (Rom 1:17).

A summary of Luther's religious conviction in 1517

(i)   Man is justified or saved by faith in Christ without the merits of good works.

(ii) Every Christian has a direct access to God through faith in Jesus Christ. No other mediation is required for salvation.

(iii) The Bible is the sole moral authority for faith and life. Traditions can have values if based on the scriptures.

(iv) God asserts His actual and full presence in the Holy Ghost. The Bible must be interpreted by illumination and with the help of the Holy Spirit.

(v)   The essence of God is love. Religion is based on God's gift of grace or God's love for the sinner. This grace is free for all and may be accepted and enjoyed by all who have faith. Consequently there is no absolute predestination.

(vi) It is the blessed privilege of every Christian to have full certainty of his or her personal salvation in Christ.

In 1517, he published his 95 Theses on Justification. Again in 1517, he published 97 Theses for improving the curriculum and methods of study at the University of Wittenberg. By this time his preaching and teaching had made him a true witness of Christ. But the reformation was born on October 31, 1517, when he nailed his 95 Theses against the sale of indulgences to the door of the Castle church in Wittenberg.

From Luther's 95 Theses to his death

Pope Leo X (1513-1521) tried to raise funds for the completion of the magnificent Church building of St. Peter in Rome by proclaiming a general sale of indulgences. Germany under Maximilian I agreed to this papal demand. Luther could not tolerate seeing many buying indulgences in spite of his warning against it. So Luther nailed his famous theses to the door of the Church in Wittenberg. Copies of these theses and a letter were sent to the Archbishop of Mainz. In a sermon to the town people, Luther called attention to his theses. The main points of his theses are:

(i)   Repentance is not an outward act but an attitude of the mind.

(ii) The Church's true treasury is God's forgiving grace.

(iii) Every sincerely repenting Christian has the right to full remission of sins without any letter from the Pope.

(iv) Christians should seek discipline and not try to avoid it.

There was a serious reaction to the Theses. Germany, on the whole, keenly supported Luther, but some theologians attacked him; and Tetzel (Salesman) and the Archbishop of Mainz made a complaint to Rome.

In 1518, he was summoned before the papal legate in Germany, who ordered him to retract his theses. Luther refused on the ground that he could not act against his conscience. He finally fled from the city.

While Rome was collecting materials to prove the heresy of Luther, he published several tracts. They include the following tracts:

(i)   "To the Christian Nobility of German Nation" (1520). This tract is a summon to Germany to unite against Rome and a platform for a reformation of the life in the Church and state.

(ii) "On the Babylonian Captivity of the Church" (1520). He attacked certain doctrines of the Church and approved of only two sacraments–baptism (*Jal Samskar*) and Lord's Supper (He denied that the mass is a sacrifice).

(iii) "The Liberty of a Christian Man" (1520). This tract emphasised the freedom of Christian men and priesthood of all believers.

(iv) "On good works." According to this tract, the noblest of all good works is to believe in Christ; all other trades and occupations are essentially good.

Luther's writings were ordered to be burned; in 1521, he himself was threatened with a ban unless he recanted within 60 days. Luther was excommunicated and a ban was placed on the places where he worked. In some places, Luther's work was burned, but in other places, Luther was warmly welcomed. A big section of Germany was in ecclesiastical rebellion against the pope.

In 1521, Charles V, the new Emperor, opened his first Diet at Worms. Luther was allowed a fair hearing at this Diet (Parliament). April 18, 1521, was the greatest day in

Luther's life. Standing before the most powerful and influential assembly in the world of that time, he gave a well-prepared speech, which made an indelible impression upon the audience. When finally asked if he would recant, he answered that he would not go against his conscience. With scriptures in his hand, Luther challenged the entire Roman Catholic Church and Holy Roman Empire of the German nation. The Pope had already ex-communicated Luther. In 1521, the emperor and the Diet of Worms put Luther under a ban of the empire, commanding his surrender to the government at the expiration of his safe conduct and forbidding all to shelter him or to read his writings.

On his way back to Wittenberg, he was seized by friendly hands and taken secretly to the Castle of the Wartburg. During the year he spent in hiding, he made his famous translation of the New Testament into German and attacked papacy.

While Luther was in Wartburg, men of more extreme views took the leadership in Wittenberg. They taught that the images should be destroyed, that there should be no pictures in the Church and that all the priests should marry. Then more extreme people attacked infant baptism. These extreme views created alarm among the princes. In 1522, Luther was requested to return to Wittenberg. After a careful study of the situation, Luther preached a series of great sermons for eight days and restored some order. A split occurred in the reforming ranks.

During 1526-27 two main ecclesiastical organisations developed on reformed lines.

In 1529, the Diet (Assembly) of Spier made a strong order that religion must not be changed and that all monastic bishops and orders must be restored to their full power and rights. The Lutheran minority in the Diet entered a protestation against this decision. And from this incident comes the word *Protestant*. In 1534, Luther completed the translation of the Old Testament.

Luther was also a great musician; he composed a service book.

Moravian Brethren

The Moravians were spiritual descendents of John Hus. From 1415 to 1620, the Moravians existed in Bohemia and Moravia and were often persecuted and driven underground. In 1620, during the Thirty Year's war, the Roman Catholics conquered Bohemia and Moravia, and more than 36,000 of the Moravian Brethren fled to other countries. They were widely scattered and within the next hundred years were often persecuted, some of them becoming absorbed into other Protestant Churches. Count Zinzendorf (Lutheran minister, belonging to a noble and pietistic family, much influenced by the spirituality in Halle where he studied for seven years) invited the Moravians to settle on his estate of Bethelsdorf in Saxony.

The Pietistic movement or great religious awakening within the protestant Churches of the 17th and 18th centuries in the continent of Europe brought the reconstruction of the Moravian Brethren under the leadership of Count Nicolaus Ludwig von Zinzendorf. The first Moravian group settled in Hernhut in 1722.

The Moravian community organised (much against the will of Zinzendorf) into an independent Church in 1742 and became known as the 'Unity of Brethren.' By 1745, the group was a fully organised Church with bishops, elders, deacons and a separate liturgy of their own. By 1749, the English Parliament recognised it. It was in England that the adherents of this community were first generally called the Moravians. They had a great missionary zeal in them. Following the missionaries to the West Indies and Greenland, a stream of missionaries went out (in the lifetime of their leader Zinzendorf) to work in Europe, Asia, Africa and North and South America. In a few years, *little Hernhut* sent out more missionaries than had gone from all of European Protestants for two centuries. They went to the hardest and most dangerous places and the most unpromising people. Everywhere they were encouraged or inspired by joyful, confident faith and by loyalty to Christ; everywhere they showed the same courage and love for men.

In the 18th century, the Moravian Brothers thus formed one of the greatest missionary movements that the world had ever seen. They were found everywhere and were prepared to go anywhere. Their sacrificial love and life can be illustrated by the following examples:

(i)   Two of their number heard of a slave colony in West Indies and voluntarily sold themselves as slaves for the rest of their lives in order to get into the island to preach the gospel to the slaves there.

(ii) Two other (brethren) heard of a leper colony in Africa where no one was allowed to enter and return, for fear that the disease might spread. They volunteered to go into the leper colony in order to present Christ to the inmates of the colony.

(iii) Peter Bohler, one of the Moravian missionaries, converted Charles Wesley. The Conversion of Charles was a divine act. Peter Bohler prayed for Charles when he was seriously ill. Bohler assured him that he was not going to die and prayed for his conversion. He was fully healed on May 21, 1738.

(iv) John Wesley went to Georgia (America) for his missionary work in 1734, but had to come back from Georgia with a heavy heart. God, however, continued to work with him. John knew that he was not converted. Peter Bohler said to John, "Preach faith until you have it." On May 24, 1738, when John was attending a Moravian Society meeting on Aldergate street where someone was reading Luther's preface to the Epistle to Roman and describing the change that God works in the heart through faith in Christ, John felt his heart strangely warmed. He felt he did trust in Christ, Christ alone, for salvation (*Moksha*), and an assurance was given to him that He (Christ) had taken away his sins and saved him from the law of sin and death.

(v) Tibet (the land of Bodh people) had been an inhospitable land for Christian missionaries. All the efforts of Catholic missionaries to enter Tibet (in the 14th, 17th, 18th and 19th centuries) were in vain.

Various Protestants worked on the eastern frontier; in Western or Lesser Tibet, Moravian missionaries had started carrying heroic and sacrificial service at several centres since the middle of 19th century. The Moravians had their mission at Poo, which had to be given up by 1925. The interior of Tibet was closed to all missionary work for many years, by order of the Tibetan government and the British government. The latter gave the Moravian missionaries permission to found their mission only on condition that they would limit their activity to the territory under British rule.

In the Spring of 1912, Sadhu Sundar Singh tried to enter the "closed" region of Greater Tibet by the same route that had been trodden by the Franciscan missionary (Desgodis, 50 years earlier). When he reached the Moravian mission at Poo, he received a cordial welcome from two missionaries there, Kunick and Marx. They helped him acquire the rudiments of the Tibetan language and provided him with a good companion in the form of an evangelist named Tarnyed Ali. The two young men tramped over the mountains till they reached the lamasery of Trashisgang, where they were welcomed very warmly.

John Welsley

The 18th century saw England rise to be the world's dominant industrial and colonial power. New social and economic rules came into being. Wealth was concentrated in a few hands, while the large masses suffered from extreme poverty. The Churches in England failed to cope with the situation. Also, they could not get involved in world-wide mission. This situation lasted for about 50 years after the revolution under William (Prince of Orange) in England. Most of the clergymen in England were worldly and selfish and were nothing more than office holders; there were some dissolute persons as well. The duties of bishops and parish ministers were largely neglected. Preaching consisted mostly of theological discussions. Little was done to fulfil the religious needs of the people, and people were out of touch with the Church. For 50 years, church life was only a cold formality; religious enthusiasm was rare; no missionary work was done.

The greatest need of the hour was a living and practical Christianity that could eradicate social evil. The prevailing moral tone was low. Drunkenness increased much in the first half of the 18th century. Poverty went on multiplying; inflation grew three times between 1714 and 1750. In the towns, crime and disorder were common, in spite of the brutal penal laws.

The Revival

It was during these troubled times that John Wesley was raised up by God to awaken the spiritual life of England and to bring a strong religious impulse into the world. John was born in 1703 in his father's rectory (Parsonage) at Empworth in England. His father (Samuel Wesley) was one of the few earnest and active men in the ministry of the Church of England at that time. His mother (Susanna Wesley) was a gifted and saintly woman with a rare combination of strict discipline, human sympathy and religious fervour. At Oxford, he distinguished himself as a scholar. His life was not without temptations, but his mother's teaching and prayers saved him from falling into outward sins. John got his M.A. degree in 1927 and was made lecturer in Greek in Oxford University. He was ordained as Priest in the Church of England in 1928. In Oxford, as Greek lecturer, he became the leader of a group of students who were very scrupulous and methodical in their observance of religious services and college duties. So they were nicknamed 'Holy Club' and the 'Methodists.' Among them were his brother Charles Wesley and George Whitefield. This 'Holy Club' encouraged like-minded students to spend their time in daily prayers and Bible study and to involve themselves in visiting prisons, helping poor families and caring for the sick. They organised themselves in such a way that every minute of the day could be profitably used. Member of the Holy Club fasted twice a week, denied their selfish lives and luxuries and practised all rules for the attainment of holiness as laid down in the *Book of Common Prayer*. They adopted a system of rules for holy living. It was this regularity of life that earned them the name "Methodist"-one who follows an exact method laid down in Holy Scriptures.

In 1735, John Wesley went to Georgia (America) as a missionary (Charles Wesley also did so in the same year) for the Indians of the newly founded colony there. But this experience was brief (1735-1937) and fruitless. At this time, he was a man of zeal. In Georgia, Wesley was kindly received and worked diligently. He organised a society patterned after the Oxford Society. He had great expectations of doing his work with the Indians but was disappointed. The people in Georgia were so well content with their manner of living that they paid no heed to Wesley's teaching. There he came in contact with some Moravian missionaries, in whom he saw a Christian confidence and joy that he had never known. This brought a big change in his religious life. His disappointment in Georgia brought him back from America to England on December 27, 1739, as a discouraged man. But the need of a change in his religious life remained alive after his return to England, under the influence of other Moravians. God was at work with Wesley. John Wesley writes, "On the 24th May 1738, I *unwillingly* attended a *Moravian Society meeting* in Aldergate Street (England) where someone was reading *Luther's Preface to the Epistle to the Romans.* While he was describing the change which God works in the heart through faith in Christ, *I felt my heart strangely warmed. I felt I did trust in Christ, Christ alone for salvation* (Moksha): *and an assurance was given to me that he (Christ) had taken away my sins, even mine, and saved me from the law of sin and death."*

Three days earlier, John's younger brother Charles had also experienced a sudden conversion, and the two brothers were now united in their desire to make their newly experienced faith known to the world. The religious revolution began in England by the preaching of the Wesleys—due to their rebirth (new life in Christ).

Turning Point

March of 1739 saw Wesley preaching outdoors to the gathering of some neglected people near Bristol, among whom George Whitefield had preached for a few weeks in 1735; he had an experience much like Wesley's conversion. Soon afterwards Whitefield became a preacher of remarkable power, drawing great crowds to listen to him. He then succeeded Wesley in Georgia. During a visit to England he preached to the forsaken colliers near Bristol, and to this field he summoned Wesley.

From this time (1739), for nearly 50 years, Wesley laboured hard. At first he worked among the helpless people in Bristol, London and Newcastle. In 1742, he began his marvellous work as an itinerant preacher. For more than 40 years, he travelled 4,000-5,000 miles a year and preached about 15 times a week. He visited all parts of England, and did much work in Scotland and Ireland. He often met with violent opposition, but remained undaunted. Wherever he preached he organised Methodist 'Societies.' To care for them, he built up his heroic company of lay preachers. He used to say, "I look upon all the World as my Parish." He travelled mostly on horseback and covered an estimated 250,000 miles and preached 40,000 sermons! His voice touched many hearts, and the words he spoke influenced many minds.

The two other powerful workers in the revival were Charles Wesley and Whitefield. Charles Wesley was an effective preacher, but he contributed mostly through the hymns he had composed. Many of the hymns composed by him have won permanent places among Christian hymns. Whitefield remained active as a travelling evangelist for many years. He did not work with Wesley because of theological differences. Whitefield was a strict Calvinist and

John Wesley was an Arminian. For fifteen years he preached forty or more times a week. Astonishing stories are told of the power of his oratory over his audiences. Unlike Wesley, he was merely a preacher and organised nothing. However, he exerted a commanding influence through his preaching.

Although the Wesleys and Whitefield were clergymen of the Church of England, they were not allowed to preach in its churches. For a long time, the Anglican clergy were almost wholly ignorant of the real nature and value of their work. Their habit of preaching in other men's parishes without permission caused great consternation. For such reasons they were excluded from the churches; and from many of the clergy they received bitter opposition or contempt.

Nevertheless, the broad movement that they started did affect the Church of England. There grew up a strong party called the "Evangelicals," which consisted of clergymen and laymen who were influenced by the revival. Of this party were John Newton, Tplady - the author of "Rock of Ages," and William Wilberforce - the great anti-slavery leader. Towards the end of the 18th century, the Evangelicals became dominant in the Church. Since many of them were people of wealth and high position, they greatly affected the life of England.

The preaching of the revival was, as Wesley said, nothing new. It was proclamation of God's free grace in Christ, of salvation through faith in Christ and of the call to repentance and faith. The hymns of the revival, such as Charles Wesley's "Jesus, lover of my soul," Cowper's "Hark, my soul, it is the Lord," and Toplady's "Rock of Ages," show the great truths that were taught and learned. This old evangelical message, which for years had been almost unknown in England, was now given with passionate earnestness.

Results of the Revival

(i) The first great result was the formation of a new church, the Methodist. Wesley did not desire that. He loved the Church of England and wished that the people who became Christians under his preaching and under his fellow workers could be taken into it. The organisation of a new Church was forced upon him. Gradually, he formed a church consisting of his societies and preachers, and in 1784, the Wesleyan, or Methodist, Church was fully organised. Seven years later, at Wesley's death, it had 77,000 members.

(ii) The spiritual awakening of England affected the nation widely and deeply. Thousands of people who had been living in practical heathenism, because of the neglect of the Church of England, were gathered into Methodist Societies. Most of them belonged to the working classes; Christianity became far more powerful in the upper classes than it had been, and a far higher moral standard ruled there. A fresh enthusiasm took possession of the English religious life, driving out the lukewarmness and dryness of the early 18th century.

(iii) The love of God, felt with new power through the preaching of the revival, stirred men to love and serve their brethren. Modern social service thus got its first powerful impetus. The first Sunday school was opened in 1780 by Roberet Raikes in Gloucester. This was one of the early steps in popular education in England, as well as the beginning of the Sunday School movement. Raike's School was for the poor children growing up in ignorance; and general education and religious instruction were given to them. Slave trade and child labour were abolished by the leadership of Wilberforce and other evangelicals. Prison reform was done by John Howard and Elizabeth Fry. Public care of the poor became more kindly and intelligent. Many hospitals and other charities were founded.

(iv) The greatest of all the effects of the revival was the rise of the modern missionary movement. The splendid honour of leadership in the awakening of missions belongs to William Carey, a cobbler and Baptist lay preacher. In the face of contemptuous opposition, he pressed on his associates his vision of the conversion of the non-Christian world. Finally, in 1792, for his noble work, William Carey as the first missionary was sent to India. The London Missionary Society was formed in 1795 (chiefly by Congregationalists), and the Church Missionary Society in 1799 (by the Evangelicals of the Church of England). All the great religious bodies of England felt the missionary inspiration by the end of the century. Their enthusiasm spread to Scotland, America and Europe

William Carey

The great spiritual revival of 1739 under the leadership of John Wesley caused the rise of the modern missionary movement. William Carey had the splendid honour of leadership in awakening of missions. In 1792, he secured the organisation of the Baptist Society for propagating the Gospel among the heathens.

William Carey came to India in the employ of the East India Company in order to get into the country, but he made missionary work here his primary concern.

William Carey, whose motto was "Expect great things from God; attempt great things for God," came to India and became a leader in the translation of the Bible into the tongue of the people, although nominally he was a Chaplain of the East India Company. He became a great social reformer and introduced many changes in India. He was instrumental in abolishing *sati*. He started the first lending library. He is the founder of Serampore University, Calcutta (now Kolkata). He published the first newspaper in all of Asia, introduced the first saving Bank in India and established the first Botanical Society in India.

The quest of his soul for union, communion and service of the Creator made him the 'Father of Modern Mission.' He expected great things from God and attempted great things for God. He also did great things for India

Mrs. Jessie Penn–Lewis

"Mrs. Jessie Penn-Lewis was a great woman of God, whose writings have led many Christians to a deeper understanding of the Cross in the believers' life. Her biography records that there was a time in her life, when after some years after serving God, she came to a place of dissatisfaction with the results of her labours. She was born again, but she realised that she needed to be filled by the Holy Spirit as well. And so she sought God's face earnestly for this. One day while in prayer, she saw a vision of a hand holding a bundle of dirty rags. A voice said, 'This is the result of all your service for Me thus far.' She was surprised. Here she was a born-again and consecrated child of God. Surely this was not a picture of her labours. But the Lord showed her that it was her *self-life* that she had consecrated to God and that self could produce only dirty rags. And then the Lord spoke to her that she needed to be crucified.

"This was difficult to accept initially. But she did. And as a result, rivers of living water began to flow through her life, bringing blessing and refreshment to thousand in many parts of the world. Truly, she inherited Abraham's blessing and people of many nations were blessed through her" (Zac Poonen: *Beauty For Ashes*,pp 58-59).

Dr. E. Stanley Jones

Dr. E. Stanley Jones (1884-1973), a twentieth-century Methodist Christian missionary and theologian and a friend of Mahatma Gandhi, started his career as a Pastor of English Church in Lucknow and became an international figure. He was the one who founded the Nur Manzil Psychiatric Centre, which still serves and caters to the needs of mental patients.

He also founded the Christian Sattal Ashram (1930) at Sattal, Nainital, which continues to serve as a beautiful retreat centre for learning, renewal and witness to Lord Jesus Christ and His kingdom. The Ashram has developed into a permanent training Centre for college students, pastors, teachers, and youth with a resident Acharya. From Sattal, the International Christian Ashram movement has spread to thirty eight countries. In 1915, when he was the Superintendent of the Methodist districts of Sitapur and Rai-Bareli, Dr. Jones was invited by Sitapur Indian club of high class people (judges, lawyers, doctors, administrators and the like) to join them. At the close of a game, the group would meet and relax and their conversation often turned to religion. A judge asked the missionary Jones why he was interested in outcastes and not in the higher castes. Jones said the high castes were not interested and so the door was open for the lower castes. The judge said, "This is a mistake. We do want you, if you come in the right way."

"Come in the right way" changed the life-ministry of Stanely Jones. "I began to see where my life-work lay" he wrote. "I had been circling and circling like a homing pigeon to find its homeward direction—circling for seven or eight years since I arrived in India. But now I felt a strange homeward pull—towards the intelligentsia of India...I had to struggle with my new mental attitudes. I had been brought up as a theological conservative...with a theological system. My mind was now free to follow the Truth wherever found. So I decided I would follow the truth wherever it led me."

Jones was the first in Methodist history who resigned as Bishop-elect of the Methodist Episcopal Church.

Now he began to study the philosophical thoughts of the great living religions, particularly Hinduism. He paid special attention to the five living seeds in Hinduism (Spirit as ultimate reality; unity in the whole universe; justice at the heart of the universe; passion for freedom [liberation]; and discipleship) and presented the Gospel with non-traditional expressions. Subsequently, he started speaking constantly to ever-growing audiences of educated people of other faiths throughout India. Many learned countrymen came to accept Jesus as Saviour through him.

Acharya R.C. Das of Varanasi

This learned convert to Christ did his best in reaching educated *Vedantis* in north India during 1908-1976.

Rajendra Chandra Das was born in East Bengal (now Bangladesh) in 1887. He did M.A. in English, Sanskrit and Philosophy and became a professor of Philosophy in St. Paul's College, Calcutta. Apart from his educational job, he introduced an indigenous form of worship in his own residence, which was attended by student inquirers, new converts and interested Church leaders every Sunday. He would often go out with professors and students to witness the Gospel in different parts of the city. Crowds listened to him. He joined the Anglican Church in 1916 and was subsequently ordained as clergyman.

The C.M.S. appointed him as an Evangelist in Kushtia (East Bengal). Just after two years of his service, he was dismissed from Mission as he had invited a Hindu lawyer to share his love for Christ in an evangelistic service. During the brief stay at Kushtia, R.C. Das had built a church for a gospel centre and had been using indigenous methods effectively. New converts arose both from Islam and Hinduism. In 1930, this professor-evangelist moved to Varanasi (one of the principal seats of sadhus, sanyasis and educated Hindus). He started a *Khristpanthi ashram* in Varanasi. Das encouraged emergence of Christian *ashrams* based on 'poverty and obedience.' He was invited to many seminars and conferences in the country. In 1932, he was invited by Dr. E. Stanley Jones to Sattal Ashram where he delivered lectures on Hinduism.

In Varanasi, he began to train people for evangelistic work using indigenous ways—for which he was accused of being anti-European and anti-Church by Mission HQ in London and was dismissed again from Mission. However, he continued with his ashram. He wrote in his periodical magazine that during the course of his long ministry in the sacred city, not less than one hundred educated Hindus followed Jesus in the *Samskara of baptism*.

In 1940, he founded a "Society for study of Hinduism," as he was convinced that a genuine study would promote mutual understanding and good will. For lack of support from mission and the Church (both moral and substantial), the society had to close down in 1957. During this period, nearly 225 students had gone through the course of study. Thereafter, due to lack of regular school for study of Hindu faith, the Church did not have leaders in Indian Christian Theology and there were not any personnel who could handle Christian *ashrams* effectively.

Acharya R.C. Das believed in the power of the written word and so for many years he edited the *Seeker*, the *Pilgrim*, etc., and gave prophetic guidance to the Church at large. He commented on many topics, ranging from Kingdom of God, the Church, indigenisation, foreign-ness in some Christian ashrams, the Christian sadhu, the Gandhian Movement, the Nyogi Commission, Church Union, World Council of Churches, anti-conversion bills and so on.

Regarding the Church and mission, he said: Here follow a few sampling of his concern on Church and Mission:

> I became a Christian, not because I found Hinduism all weak or false or bad, but because I found its strength, its truth and its goodness not strong, true and good enough as my soul in utter need demanded.

> All thoughtful people know, Hinduism with all its faults is very much nearer to true Christianity than is either Islam or western materialism.

> We have not met with any hostility or discourtesy during our 27 years in connection with our witness in the midst of orthodox Hindus.

> In the early and pioneering days of Missions great converts like Dr. K.M. Banerjee, Lal Behari Dey, K.C. Banerjee, B. Chakravarty, Mathuranath Bose, Sushil Kumar Rudra, Br. Upadhyaya, latterly prof. Serajuddin, Rev. Ahmad Shah, Rev. B.B. Roy, Principal J.R. Banerjee, and Madhusudan Das were there with great original talent and power. Except that some of them were given some high positions and that under Mission control they were never encouraged or given scope to use their powers and abilities-Spiritual, evangelistic, literary or administrative, to the end of making the Church autonomous, So their work and ability bore no permanent fruit. At the end of a century we have a divided, poor, superficial church, unrelated to the country. It was due again to the lack of foresight, unwillingness to pay the cost, and a desire for domination–hindrances which still exist today.

R.C. Das, the evangelical prophet of his time, passed away in 1976 unto his eternal reward. "His was a lonely voice against much of the prevailing wisdom of his day" (*With Christ in India in the New Millennial Year* by Acharya Daya Prakash).

Mother Teresa

She established homes for the dying people in the streets of Calcutta; she established homes for old people; she established 81 centres for lepers; she won the Nobel Prize and other medals. The reason for winning prizes: Jesus Christ. She saw Jesus in the destitute.

Pandita Ramabai

Born in an orthodox Brahmin home, she was well versed in Sanskrit and Hindu scriptures. She started *Sarada Sadan* to provide for and teach widowed women. She also built Mukti Mission at Kedgaon, Pune.

Ida Sophia Scudder

She started village health centres and a nursing college for women. Also, she was the founder of the Christian Medical College and Hospital, Vellore.

Amy Carmichael

She established a home for small girls in Dohnavur. Also, she sought *deevadasi* children with love and wrote more than 35 books. She is appreciated for her sixty years of service in Tamil Nadu.

William Goudie

He stood for the cause of the poor and oppressed and liberated many *dalits* in and around Thiruvellore, Tamil Nadu. Village schools, health care of the marginalised, emancipation of women and women's education were some of his main concerns.

Bartholomaeus Ziegenbalg

His creations include the first Tamil dictionary, Tamil grammar books, the first translation of the New Testament into Tamil, the first calendar, the first hymn book and the first girls' school. He also set up a printing press.

Henry Martin

He translated the New Testament into Urdu. Educated in Cambridge, he mastered Hindi, Persian and Arabic and started a school for women. He is also known for sharing the Gospel with beggars.

Alexander Duff

Started English language schools in India, initiated schools for women from the High caste society and tried to create an awareness of the social evils of the day.

St. Thomas

He is regarded as the patron saint of India. An apostle to India, he came to Punjab in 46A.D. and then moved to south India (Chennai) in 52 A.D. He established churches in Kerala and Tamilnadu and died as a martyr while working near Mylapur, Chennai, in 72 A.D. The famous St. Thomas Mount in Chennai is a monument to him.

Sadhu Sundar Singh

Born on September 3, 1889, at Rampur, Patiala, Punjab, Sundar Singh came from a wealthy aristocratic Sikh family. His mother was a wonderfully religious woman who was the best spiritual guide for him from his very childhood. Every morning he had to read portions from the Vedas and Shastras, the Granth and the Bhagvad-Gita before having his milk. At the age of seven he had learnt the Bhagvad-Gita by heart. His mother used to say to him, "You must not be superficial and worldly like your brothers. You must seek peace of soul and love religion, and one day you will become a holy Sadhu." His whole inner life became a great longing for *shanti* (peace of soul). And when at last he found it, he fulfilled his mother's desires by becoming a sadhu. Sundar Singh later said that his mother would have become a Christian if she had lived longer.

Sundar Singh was the apostle of the East and the West. He was a messenger of God. He firmly believed that he who lives in Christ becomes dead to sin and enters eternal life.

In his work, *Gospel of Sadhu Sundar Singh*, Prof F. Heiler writes:

> At the early age of 14, Sundar Singh lost his mother, at the time when his *religious conflicts* had already begun. Deep sorrow filled his heart, a sorrow which left its marks upon him. His religious conflicts increased in him a great zeal for reading sacred books. He often sat until midnight reading the Granth, the Upanishads, and the Koran. He learnt by heart a great many passages. He tormented himself so much over religious questions because he wanted to have peace at all costs. The things of this world could not satisfy him at all. Besides this strenuous study, he used to practise concentrated meditation for hours at a time; but even this effort brought him no inward peace. Under the guidance of a Hindu Sanyasi he learnt the practice of Yoga. By means of prolonged concentration he succeeded in producing a *trance-state* which brought him temporary relief; but when he returned to normal consciousness he found that he was exactly where he was before the Yoga exercises began.

The counsel and instructions that he received from Indian *purohitas* (priest) and sadhus were powerless to give him any help along the path towards peace of heart.

To put it in the words of Sundar Singh, "I tried to find rest through the means offered by the religions of India: Hinduism, Buddhism, Mohammedanism (Islam) ; but I could not find it there... I wanted to save myself. How I studied all our sacred books! How I strove for peace and rest of the soul! I did good works. I did all that could lead to peace, but I did not find it, for I could not achieve it for myself."

At the mission school of his native place, he had refused to read the New Testament. He thought: "There may possibly be good things in this book, but it is against our religion." Sundar's hatred of Christianity grew so strong that he became a ring leader of a group of pupils who declared themselves the "enemies of Christianity." Again and again he tore up and burnt portions of the Bible and other Christian writings. But in spite of this fanatical hatred the mysterious book of the Christians would not leave him alone. "Even then," he confessed, "I felt the Divine attractiveness and wonderful power of the Bible...I felt its refreshing effects upon my soul." Above all, it was the word of Jesus which had begun to speak to the depth of his restless, longing soul: "Come unto Me, all Ye that are weary and heavy laden, and I will give you rest...and ye shall find rest ..." The other words that pierced his soul were, "God so loved the world that He gave His only begotten Son, that whosoever believeth in Him should not perish, but have everlasting life." But he could not truly grasp these messages. He thought, "Christ could not save Himself, how can He save others."

In order to disprove or confute these mysterious words, he made a deep study of the religious writings of his own land. He compared them with the New Testament but could find no one who could say as Jesus did, "I will give you rest." The conflict between Christianity and Hinduism enraged him so much that he burnt the Bible— that mysterious book which promised peace but brought with it nothing but restlessness and conflict. Memory of the day on which he burnt the Bible never left him. He says, "The remembrance that I have persecuted Christ and torn up the Bible is like a perpetual thorn in my memory."

At last the inward restlessness and unhappiness of Sundar Singh made him so desperate that he decided to commit suicide, in the hope that he would find rest in the other world. He said, "If I cannot find God in this world, perhaps, I can find him in the other."

One early morning, after taking a ceremonial cold bath, he began to plead with God to show him the way to achieve salvation. As his soul was full of doubts, he prayed at first "like an atheist": "O God, if there be a God, show me the right way, and I will become a sadhu; otherwise I will kill myself." He prayed and prayed without stopping; he besought God earnestly to deliver him from this uncertainty and unrest and to give him peace, but there was no answer. He continued to strive with God in prayer in the hope of finding peace.

Suddenly a great light shone in his little room. He thought the house was on fire, so he opened the door and looked out; there was no fire there. He closed the door and went on praying.

Then he saw a wonderful vision: in the centre of a luminous cloud he saw the face of a Man, radiant with love. At first he thought it was Buddha or Krishna, or some other divinity, and he was about to prostate himself before it. Just then, to his great astonishment, it began to speak in Hindustani: *Tu mujhe kyun satata hai? Dekh main ne tere liye apni jan salib par di* (Why do you persecute Me? Remember that I gave My life for you upon the Cross). Then he noticed the scars of Jesus of Nazareth on that kind man. Sundar Singh fell at His feet and worshipped Him. He felt his whole being change; Christ flooded his nature with Divine life; peace and joy filled his soul and "brought heaven into his heart." When Sundar Singh rose from his knees Christ had disappeared, but the wonderful peace remained from that moment. He said afterwards: "Neither in Hindustani, my mother-tongue, nor in English, can I describe the bliss of that hour."

Full of joy, he roused his father, exclaiming "I am a Christian!" Explaining the miraculous happening to his father, Sundar said, "Because I have seen Him. Until now I always said, 'He is simply a man who lived two thousand years ago.' But today I have seen Him Himself, the living Christ, and I intend to serve Him, for I have felt His power. He has given me the peace which no one else could give. Therefore, I know that He is the living Christ. I will, and I must serve Him." Then his father said, "But just now you were going to kill yourself." The boy replied, "I have killed myself: The old Sundar Singh is dead; I am a new being."

This vision of Christ brought Sundar the fulfilment of his passionate longing and anguished striving: Shanti—that wonderful peace, "the peace which passes all understanding...heaven upon earth." Sundar Singh is quoted saying, "After I had wearied myself out in searching through Hinduism at last I found in Christ the rest and peace which my soul desired." Sundar Singh regards his conversion as a direct revelation, a "miracle" in the strict sense of the term, something absolutely supernatural. In 1920, he said:

What I saw was no imagination of my own. It was no dream...It was a reality, the living Christ! He can turn an enemy of Christ into a preacher of the Gospel. He has given me His peace, not for a few hours merely, but throughout sixteen years (w.e.f. 18th Dec. 1904)–a peace so wonderful that I cannot describe it, but can testify its reality.

That which other religions could not do for many years Jesus did it in few seconds. He filled my heart with infinite peace.

Neither reading nor books brought about the change ... it is Christ Himself who has changed me.

When He revealed Himself to me I saw His glory, and knew that He was the living Christ.

Expressing his views about Sundar's conversion, F. Heiler, Professor of History of Religions, University of Marburg, Germany, says, "Sundar Singh sees in his conversion a manifestation of the transcendental God, a revelation of the living Christ. Indeed he emphsises the objectivity of his experience of Christ to such an extent that he separates this vision from others which have been granted to him during ecstasy (as, for instance during his fast). To Prof. Hardon of Berne he said clearly, 'I have had visions, and I know how to distinguish them, but Jesus I have only seen once.' For him, as for the apostles, the Risen Christ is an objective, concrete reality."

After finding his Saviour, Sundar Singh spent several days in solitary prayer. In fervent prayer, he besought God for forgiveness; then he received from the Lord the assurance of his forgiveness.

The first witness given by the fifteen-year-old Sundar Singh to his Saviour was his steadfast courage in confessing Christ to his family and friends. In his own family, he had to endure scorn, mockery and persecution. His former companions reproached him as a perjurer, renegade and deceiver; his own brother persecuted him with bitter hatred. His newly converted friend, Gurdit Singh, and all the Christians of the village had to leave the district. Now Sundar Singh's life was in danger, and he sought refuse at the Presbyterian mission school at Ludhiana. Here he had his first painful experiences among Christians; his fellow-pupils were mostly nominal Christians who did not live according to the teaching of Christ. Disappointed, he left the mission school and returned to his own family. But his faith in the Redeemer was not shattered. His family tried to persuade him to keep his Christian faith secret, but this temptation was overcome when he heard a voice saying to him, "He who confesses Me before men will I confess him before the face of My Father in Heaven." And he obeyed the voice. Sundar confessed Christ fearlessly before them all and made a complete break with the Sikh community by cutting off his long hair. From this time onward, his family treated him as an outcast. He had to sleep and eat outside the house. Finally, his father disinherited him and drove him away from home. Taking nothing with him except his New Testament and a little parcel of provisions, the sixteen-year-old Sundar Singh began to tread the `Way of Homelessness." His soul was flooded with wonderful peace. The Sadhu says, "That was my first night in Heaven. The world could not give me such peace. Christ, the living Lord, breathed into me glorious peace. The cold pierced me through and through, I was a hungry outcast, but I had the sense of being enfolded in the power of the 'Living Christ.' The presence of my Redeemer turned suffering into joy."

Sundar Singh was guided by God to go to the Christians at *Rupar*. As soon as he reached the house of the Presbyterian missionary, Mr. Uppal, he broke down completely. The poison in the sweet dish given to him by one of his relatives had begun to work. His friend, Gurdit Singh, had already died of the poison given to him by his father. The doctor attending Sundar in this critical situation left him with little hope of recovery. But his Saviour was with him; he was soon fully recovered. Thereafter, he returned to the Christian Boys' Boarding School at Ludhiana, where the missionaries (Dr. Wherry and Dr. Fife) took adequate care of him. Later, for his safety, he was sent to Subathu, a medical mission station near Shimla. There in quietness he studied the Bible and prepared himself for baptism.

After his conversion, Sundar Singh obeyed the call of his Master to bear witness to the power and love of his Saviour. Then he remembered the words of his mother: "One day you will be a *sadhu*." He decided to become a Christian sadhu, an evangelist in the yellow robe of an Indian ascetic (sanyasi). He preferred the ideal of his countrymen and wished to preach the Gospel as a wandering sadhu. So thirty-three days after his baptism, the young Christian wore the sacred yellow robe and made a vow to be a sadhu for the rest of his life.

So, the sixteen-year-old boy went out to his missionary wanderings, bare-footed, with no possessions, without any protection against the wild beasts. He had a thin linen garment, a blanket, which he often used as a turban, and a copy of the New Testament in his mother tongue. He never begged; he depended upon the alms given to him by kind-hearted people; if these were withheld, he satisfied his hunger with roots and leaves. If kindly people received him into their houses, he accepted the hospitality gratefully. If he found no shelter, he would sleep in a dirty inn, or even a cave, or under the trees. His Hindu fellow-countrymen often gladly gave him food and shelter. Sometimes, he took refuse in the jungle, where he would pass the night hungry and shivering. Sundar Singh used to go to shrines where pilgrims congregated, where he would preach the Gospel to the sadhus and sanyasis. At first, the Sadhu preached the Gospel in his native place and in the neighbouring villages; then he wandered, preaching, through the Punjab to Afghanistan and Kashmir. After a long and tiring missionary tour, he returned to *Kotgarh* (a small place near Shimla) in order to rest. There he joined the American missionary, Mr. Stokes, who belonged to a wealthy family and had come to India to preach the Gospel like a Franciscan friar. Following the Sadhu's example, he also wore (donned) the yellow robe of the ascetic. In 1907, both gave themselves to the work in the leper asylum at Subathu, and to the care of the sick in the plague hospital at Lahore. In 1909, the Sadhu joined a theological college at Lahore and in 1910, he left the seminary, having received a licence to preach in the Anglican Churches of the diocese of Lahore. But the Sadhu could not manage to confine himself within the limits of Anglican preaching activity. Like John Wesley, he regarded the whole world as his parish, and preached everywhere and to all who would receive his message.

At the end of 1912, he had a desire to fast for 40 days in the desert, believing that in this way he would become more deeply conformed to Christ inwardly and that this would lead to greater Christ-likeness of life. His physical health declined rapidly; his sight and hearing became dim; his spiritual life, on the contrary, became increasingly full of clearness and liberty; in a state of *ecstatic concentration* he lived entirely in the supernatural world. While his body was helpless and without feeling, his soul experienced the deepest peace and the most wonderful happiness. The fast had renewed and strengthened him inwardly. Temptations, hindrances and perplexities, which had previously troubled him, had all disappeared. During his 10 to 12 days' fasting in the jungle, he was convinced that the soul was independent of the body and that the wonderful peace that he enjoyed was the result of Divine presence.

Sundar Singh chose Tibet—the stronghold of Buddhism—to preach the Gospel. He knew neither the language, nor the country, nor the people; he only knew the difficulties in his way were very great. But for his love for Christ, his zeal for the Gospel and his readiness to lay down his life for Christ, he set out for this apparently impossible work. In the spring of 1912, he tried to enter the "closed" region of Greater Tibet taking the same route used by the Franciscan missionary 50 years earlier. When he reached the Moravian mission station at Poo he received a cordial welcome from two missionaries there (Kunick and Marx). They lent him an evangelist (Tarnyed Ali) as a companion. The two young men tramped over the mountains till they reached the lamasery of Trashisgang, where they were welcomed very kindly.

After that, Sundar Singh seems to have wandered about alone for a while in the land of Bodh (Tibet). Every year the Sadhu went up to the Himalayas and tried to cross the border.

The Sadhu's reception in Tibet was not always a hostile one; on the contrary, he was often met with friendliness and kindness. In this inhospitable land, too, Sundar Singh found friends and helpers. He, however, encountered bitter hostility among the Tibetan lamas. Sundar Singh used to say, "When I go to Tibet I never expect to return. Each time I think it will be last; but it is the Will of God that I am preserved."

They also used to have continual trouble getting food for themselves. Only tea, which was drunk with salt and butter, and parched barley were provided. "Sometimes," writes the Sadhu, "the barley is prepared in such a way that even a horse or a mule will not touch it. There is only one comfort in the midst of all these troubles. They are all endured for the sake of the cross. For my sake, Christ left heaven and endured the suffering of the cross. If I, for His sake, in order to save souls, have left India and have come to Tibet, that is no great matter. But if I did not go, that would be sad indeed, for it was surely my duty to go... and we had good opportunities of preaching in other villages. But the people were very few in number; thieves and robbers also abound, keeping the countryside in a state of panic...a dreadful place to live in, where many people had been murdered... In that panic stricken area, I preached the Word of God. Indeed, those very robbers who had committed murders came in and stayed with us, and did not do us the least bit of harm...the Lord brought us through in safety." The Sadhu noticed that in spite of their addiction to violence, and their dirty way of living, the Tibetans were at heart a very kindly and religious folk.

The Sadhu made several missionary journeys in Nepal as well. As Nepal was the stronghold of Mahayana Buddhism, Christian missions were unable to find a footing there. Here, too, the Sadhu was persecuted for his faith; here too, by God's providence, he received frequent support form the secret order of Christian *sanyasis*.

From the year 1912 the fame of the Sadhu spread throughout the whole of India. Sundar Singh went through India "like a magnet." Wherever he went Christians and people of other faiths came to see him. In the beginning of 1918, he went to Madras (Chennai). He was requested to do evangelistic work in South India among the communities that were at that time deprived of the German missionaries on account of the war; so he stayed and worked for some time in that region. Until May 1918 the Sadhu worked in South India; then he went to Ceylon for six weeks. Sundar Singh spoke severely to the Christians of Ceylon about their spirit of caste, wealth and luxury, which he considered the greatest hindrance to the spread of the Gospel in that land. In July 1918, he returned to South India and then went to Calcutta, Bombay, Burma, Penang, Singapore, Japan, etc., preaching the Gospel everywhere and bearing witness to the great things God had done for him.

> In July 1919, he came to North India and got ready for his evangelical work in *Lesser Tibet* (Spite) through Subathu and Kotgarh along with a Tibetan named Tarneyed Ali who had already served him as an interpreter. When he returned from this journey a great joy was given him. His father received him kindly, and asked him the Way to Christ. The Sadhu recommended him to read the Bible and to pray. His father did so, and after some time he said to his son: "I have found thy saviour. He has become my saviour too." After this his father paid expenses of his journey to Europe, which had long been a desire of the Sadhu.

According to Heiler, one reason of the Sadhu's journey was the accusation so often brought by strict Hindus against the West—that European Christianity had had its day and had lost its influence over the life of Western nations. He wished to find out for himself whether these charges were justified, for in his mission work (in the East) they were a constant hindrance. The immediate reason, however, was—as always in the life of the Sadhu—a special call from God. The Sadhu said, "One night while I was at prayer I received a call to preach in England."

"In February 1920, he arrived at Liverpool, reached *Birmingham* (preached in several colleges and at St. John's Church in Oxford). In *London*, he preached to great crowds of all kinds of denominations (Anglican Churches, Congregationalists and Baptists, etc.). He went over to Paris at the invitation of Paris Missionary Society, and then went to Ireland and Scotland, where, in Edinburgh and Glasgo, he spoke in the leading Presbyterian Churches.

"In May (1920), he went to *America* where he gave his testimony in various ways at many of the great towns and cities like New York, Baltimore, Pittsburg, Brookyn, Philadelphia, Chicago and San Francisco. During his tour he took great pains to counteract the influence of various Hindu and Buddhist wandering preachers who had already gained a good many adherents in America to the religions of the Orient.

"On July 30th, 1920, he embarked for Australia. In Honolulu, he addressed a mixed audience, consisting of Hawaiians, Filipinos, Japanese, Chinese, English, and Americans. In Sydney, where he stayed for a week, he preached in the Cathedral as well as in all kinds of Churches, Chapels and lecture-rooms. In Melbourne, he spoke in a congregational Church. In other towns (like Perth, Adelaide, and Freemantle), the Sadhu preached in various united gatherings. In September, he landed at Bombay and hastened at once to Subathu, (at the foot of the Himalayas) took some rest and in December (1920), again took up his apostolic work, and went preaching through Punjab and Bengal.

"In the Spring of 1921, he wandered about in lonely and dangerous places, through the wilderness of the highlands of Tibet. Now he proclaimed the message in the dirty streets of Tibetan villages and towns.

"After his return from Tibet once more he preached the Word of God in his native land. The following year, he decided to accept the previous numerous invitations which he had received while in Europe. And made a second journey to Europe. He wished to visit the Holy Land also (to fulfil his long-cherished desire to visit the Holy Places connected with his Master he loved). His father, wishing to give him pleasure, again gave him the money for the journey. On 29th of January (1922) he embarked and went to Port Said; whence he went straight on to Palestine. There he visited all the places connected with the life of our Lord: Jerusalem (where he preached in Anglican Cathedral), Jordon (in which he bathed) and all other places where his Lord had lived and suffered and revealed Himself as the risen Lord. Here he found his 'Practical commentary on the Gospels.' At every step the sense of His immediate, personal presence filled his consciousness. 'He is with me wherever I go; He walks at my right hand.' His soul overflowed with joy, and tears of thankfulness were often in his eyes. And when he knelt and prayed in the Garden of Gethsemane on the Mount of Olives, it seemed as though Jesus were standing by him saying, as he said to His disciples long go: "Peace be with you. As My Father has sent Me, even so send I you.'"

From Palestine he went to places like Cairo and Marseilles to preach. Then he went to Switzerland. Here he spoke in different reformed churches in Lausanne, Geneva, Neuchatel, Berne, Thun, Basle, Zurich, St. Gall, Tavannes and other places. In Geneva he bore witness to the Living Christ in the hall in which the League of Nations met, and said, "The League of Nations has made great efforts, but it will achieve nothing until there is a league of human hearts, as such a league is only possible when men give their hearts to Him who is the Master of all hearts."

In Germany, he visited Halle, Leipzig, Berlin, Hamburg and Kiel; in Leipzig and in Kiel he also spoke at the University. He was very happy when he reached Wittenberg (the cradle of Reformation); he saw the house in which Martin Luther had lived and the Church in which he used to preach. The Sadhu spoke in this church.

In Sweden, he spoke in many towns and smaller places. At Stockholm, he was the guest of Prince Oscar Bernadotte, to whom he became attached for his faith.

From Sweden he went to Norway and Denmark. At Copenhagen, he visited the former Russian Empress at the royal palace. In Herning and Tingler, he spoke to huge audiences like those of the Syrian Church in South India. Then he travelled to Holland, where he spoke at various places.

In July (1922), the Sadhu arrived in England, quite exhausted by his labours. He had already refused pressing invitations to visit Finland, Russia, Greece, Rumania, Serbia, Italy, Portugal, America, New Zeland and England. He needed some quiet and rest. So he went to his native hills (north India) in August of 1922.

Many prominent Indians, including religious leaders, had visited Europe, the most noteworthy being Rabindranath Tagore. Almost all of them brought the message of India's religious wisdom to the intellectual world of the West. And when they talked of a synthesis of Indian and Western cultures, they were never weary of extolling the religious treasures of their native land, above all, the Upanishads, and of exhorting their Western hearers to study them. Even Brahmabandhava Upadhyay, the Christian ascetic, in his English addresses, used to praise the Indian caste system as an ideal social system and the philosophy of the Vedanta as the ideal foundation for the doctrines of the Christian revelation. Vasvani, the professor from Bombay, gave a wonderful address on "The Message of Modern India to the West" at the World Congress for Free Christianity and Religious Progress held in Berlin in 1910. He said:

> Present day India has a message for the world. The services which the West has rendered to India are well known; but it is little realised that India also has something to offer to the West; it gives access to sources of inspiration which the world needs today... The West will turn reverently to the East in order to learn its ancient wisdom, to develop its mystical sense,...to practise meditation, to learn the spirit of idealism, and in order to find the presence of God in social life.

But when Sadhu Sundar Singh came to the West he did not praise the sacred writings of his country. On the contrary, he confessed that these scriptures could not give him peace; an Indian who proclaims with all possible earnestness and exclusiveness that Christ is the Way, the Truth and the Life; that in Him dwelleth the fullness of the Godhead bodily; that the New Testament is the Word of God; and that prayer is the Way to enter heaven. Prof. F. Heiler says that this was an unheard-of thing. It was no wonder that the educated classes in Europe received this man (the Sadhu) with the greatest astonishment. The impression that the Sadhu made upon his hearers, as well as upon those who came into closer touch with him in Europe, was a deep one.

When he preached in St. Bride's Church, London, at the close "almost everyone in the congregation knelt down and prayed, a thing which was quite unusual in such meetings." Everyone felt, as the *Church Times* expressed it, that "a man from another world was speaking to them." Men and women of most varied professions, classes and countries agreed in testifying to the deep impressions made upon them both by his appearance and words.

An English theologian wrote, "I cannot say here, as I would like to do, what I feel. I have the impression of an outstanding man, who has renounced great possessions, exulting in the saving power of his Master, and one who speaks with utmost simplicity."

A Dutch theologian wrote in a private letter, "It was a revelation to me and seeing him has made the world of the New Testament more living and real."

A Swedish friend wrote about him, "It was indeed a great experience. I bowed my spirit before the great apostle because I no longer saw him, but only God, whom he proclaimed."

Countless Western theologians, who met him first with a certain reserve and mistrust, lost all their misgivings at the first encounter. Even learned men who were hostile or indifferent to Christianity were changed by the power of his personality. A professor of an English University, who had been an agnostic, said to the Sadhu, "It is not your preaching which has converted me, it is yourself; you, an Indian, are so like Christ in spirit and in bearing; you are a living witness to the Gospel and to the person of Jesus Christ."

In thousands of Christian hearts in Europe, Sundar Singh had left an indelible impression; for thousands his preaching had meant an urge (inner compulsion) to a renewed Christian life. To him, however, his visit to Western lands brought bitter disappointments; he came to realise that the idealistic notions that he had held about Western Christians were not founded on fact, and that his Hindu opponents were right when they spoke of the decadence (falling away) of Western Christianity and of the superiority of Indian inwardness and spiritual culture. The pain that this unexpected experience brought him appears in his addresses again and again.

He said, "I used to think that the inhabitants of these countries were all wonderful people; when I saw the love of God in their hearts and what they do for us, I thought they must be living Christians. But when I travelled through these lands I altered my opinion. I found things quite otherwise. Without doubt there are true servants of God in these countries, but not all are Christians. I beg to compare the inhabitants of heathen lands with those of Christendom. The former are heathen because they worship idols made with hands; in the so-called Christian lands, however, I found a worse kind of heathenism; people worship themselves. Many of them go to the theatre instead of praying and reading the Word of God; they give way to drink and to all kinds of sins. I began to realise that no European country can be called really Christian but that there are individual Christians."

Sadhu's travel in the West received the praises of thousands. He was often honoured as a saint, but he overcame this temptation as well; his deep humility remained unscathed. He remained the same humble religious soul whose only desire was to come nearer and nearer to the Lord and to grow more and more like Him; and who longed to wear himself out in His service. When he spoke of his own wonderful experiences, it was always with the thought of "exulting in Christ."

After the bitter disappointment with the West, this messenger of God turned into a severe preacher of Judgment in the eschatological sense. Then he shook off the dust of Europe from his feet and returned to his native land, with the firm resolve never to go back to the West. "This is the first and the last time that you will ever see me," he said to his hearers over and over again. He recognised that Western people–to a large extent because of greed and love of pleasure–were rejecting the message of Christ, while the people of the East, desiring truth and salvation, were embracing the Gospel of joy. So, soon after his return, he again took up the painful, laborious work of missionary tours in Tibet. In an address he gave in Switzerland, he said:

> I feel no fear at the thought of one day dying in Tibet. When that day comes I shall welcome it with joy". Each year I go back to Tibet, and perhaps even next year you will hear that I have lost my life there. Do not think 'He is dead', but say: 'He has entered Heaven and Eternal Life; he is with Christ in the perfect life.

The Sadhu read his Bible and spoke to his friends, like C.F. Andrews, about the joy it gave him. He saw God in the face of Jesus Christ. He did not come to the idea of God through the Old Testament, for he rarely studied the Psalms and the Prophets. He gave a lot of importance to the Gospels. He knew the Gospel story of Jesus by heart; it lived in his mind and fashioned his daily thoughts.

Once the Sadhu was suffering acutely from ulcer in his eye; he could do no other work, so he spent the time in prayer and intercession; the Spiritual world was opened to him and he found himself surrounded by many angels. Forgetting his pain, he asked: Do the angels and saints always look upon the face of God, and if they see Him in what form does He appear?

"One of the saints said, "As the sea is full of water so is the whole universe filled with God...because He is infinite;

His children, who are finite, can see Him only in the form of Christ."

Christ had revealed to Sundar Singh the *fullness of Divine Life*. Jesus had brought God near to him in human form. Therefore, every detail of that form was studied by the disciple with intense and rapt devotion.

He wanted to make an immediate pilgrimage to the Holy Land, walk along the very road where Jesus had walked and pray on the Mount of Olives at the very spot where Christ had prayed. When he set his foot in Palestine at last, his highly sensitive nature was stirred to its very depths. The living Christ was by his side and he was conscious of His presence.

Once he went out into wilderness to *keep a fast* just like Jesus. In the jungle, he gave himself to prayer and meditation which he wished to continue for 40 days, but he broke down after a few days. Some woodcutters found him in the jungle half-dead, so they brought him down to Rishikesh. He kept this fast to find out whether the *inner peace of the soul*, which he enjoyed as a Christian, was independent of the body; and he found that it was really independent of the body. Before he kept this fast, he was sometimes tempted into giving up the life of a Sadhu with its hardships, going back to the luxury of his father's house, getting married, and living a life of communion with God there as well; but after keeping this fast, he was able to overcome all such temptations.

Sundar Singh taught in parables. Here again his first thought was to follow literally in the footsteps of his Master. As Christ went about the villages of Galilee, so the Sadhu went about the villages in Punjab and in Shimla hills. Christ said, "My words are "Spirit" and "life." The Sadhu said that the Bible was his Guide and Light and food for his soul and that he had found his Saviour to be exactly the same as recorded in the New Testament. Like his Master he withdrew constantly into the solitude of the hills where far from his brethren, he spent hours in deep communion with the Eternal Father. And like Him, the Sadhu was full of love for children.

During 1923-1924 he did not succeed in entering Tibet. In 1925, the Sadhu nearly lost sight in one eye; he also suffered much from some kind of heart disease. In December 1925, he was dangerously ill and was unable to do evangelical work. During the days of his illness, he occupied himself with writing two valuable books, namely *Meditations* and *Visions.*

According to C.F. Andews, "After 1924 a considerable degree of heart discomfort followed almost all his public meetings. On several occasions the heart attacks were so severe to leave him unconscious for hours at a time. On his attempt to go to Tibet in 1927 a very severe haemorrhage from the stomach made his Tibetan fellow travellers take him back to the railway. While he appeared to be a little stronger in the spring of 1928, he took active part in the Bareilly Christian Convention and he remained very weak throughout the year...Just as he had expected death on his previous journey in 1927, and had quoted to his friends the verses from the Acts of the Apostles (Acts 20: 24-25), so he looked forward to death again in 1929. He felt sure that afflictions awaited him, and anticipated that those who loved him should "see his face no more." He went "bound in the spirit" unto that "jerusalem" which he was seeking with such earnestness in Tibet."

The Sadhu was admired by many.

Mary Simpson (nurse at St. Catherine's hospital, Kanpur; 1912) wrote to her sister:

He (the Sadhu) has the same calm and happy face. It is calm, and yet so intensely full of life. As he spoke about Christ revealing God's love to sinful men, his voice softened, his face changed, his eyes glowed and his whole countenance was lighted up with brightness. It was not so much his sermon-nothing could have been simpler than that; it was rather the Sadhu himself who attracted us as he brought Christ's living presence with him. Whenever I look at him; as he speaks from the Pulpit, I never have the least difficulty in knowing that he has seen Christ. My difficulty is to believe all the time that it is not Christ Himself who is speaking to us.

On another occasion, Miss Simpson met him at Kotgarh where again he preached about Christ and His constraining love. He took as his text the words of Jn 16:24: "Hitherto Ye have asked nothing in my name. Ask and ye shall receive, that your joy may be full." His message seemed to come straight form Christ Himself and to give her just what she needed most. He made those present realise that everything was possible through prayer. Then he spoke about the visions that Christ gives to His own followers — inner visions that are so bright and glorious that no amount of persecution can take away the joy and peace which comes when Christ is thus present in the inmost heart.

"The whole force of his preaching," she wrote, "seemed to rest in one strong conviction of Christ's love, which was the burden of his message. He is the one who *knows*: one who *sees* Christ face to face...Now, after seeing and hearing him, I know that everything is possible. Today I have seen what man can become like, if he truly lives in Christ. For the Sadhu is very like Christ — even his face shows it; and his presence sheds it round about him, wherever he goes. It has indeed been wonderful to have met him.

"Once he stood as a strange guest before the door of an English house. He was a tall, upright figure in a long safron-coloured robe, with a large turban bound round his head. His olive complexion and his black beard proclaimed his Indian birth; his dark eyes, with their gentle expression, revealed a heart at rest, and they shone with an infinite kindness. The stranger gives his name to the girl who opens the door: Sadhu Sundar Singh. The girl gazes at him for a moment in astonishment, then she hastens to call her mistress: 'There is someone at the door who wishes to see you, ma'am; I cannot pronounce his name, but he looks like Jesus Christ.'

"At a meeting in a certain town in America a three-year-old child was sitting in the front row. She was staring with all her might at the speaker–that mysterious man in the saffron robe. When the speaker had finished his address and had sat down, the little girl said in a clear, high voice, which rang through the hall, 'Is he Jesus Christ?'

"Many men and women, both in Asia and in Europe, who had the good fortune to see him felt as though he were a reincarnation of one of the great men of God from Bible days."

"Wherever he goes you hear people saying: 'How like he is to Christ!'" writes Mrs. Parkar, his friend and biographer. And Jean Fleury, a missionary among the Mahrattas, says: "The man is a living sermon: I have never met anyone who helps you to see Christ as he does." Even Frank Buchman, the well-known American theologian (Hartford Theological Seminary), sums up his impression of the Sadhu in these words: "He is more like Christ than anyone we have ever seen."

A Swiss minister said: "I believe that right down the centuries no one has been more like Paul than the Sadhu, in his message, as well as in other ways, not because he happens to be an oriental, but because like Paul, he is possessed by Christ to an unusual degree."

"At every turn," says the Swiss Pastor, "the New Testament comes alive in all its varied wealth of inner and outer experience; through him we see it among us in all its richness and wonder."

Dr. Nathan Soderblom–a Lutheran Archbishop of Uppsala–said: "He radiates peace and joy. One who went about with him a good deal describes him as the embodiment of peace, gentleness, and loving kindness" (cf Jn 14:27; Phil 4:7; Gal 2:20).

Mrs. Parker, his friend and biographer, said, "That which is so surprising about the Sadhu is the quite extraordinary joy which one can see upon his face–no picture can give an idea of the beauty of his smile."

It was this steady, quiet joy which particularly struck Sunder Singh's father, who had known him only as a restless, unhappy youth. In 1920, he said to his son: "I have been watching your life and comparing it with the years which you spent at home. At home you were never happy, but now, in spite of your many sorrows I have never seen you unhappy. Why is that?" Sundar answered, "It is not due to any good in me, but it has come to me because I have found peace in the Living Christ, whom formerly I hated."

Peace and joy filled the Sadhu's soul not only during periods of quiet work, but still more in times of distress, suffering and persecution. He says, "I have experienced more joy during persecution than when things went easily" (Cf Mt 5:11-12). Over and over again, as Sundar Singh tells in his addresses, it was just at the hardest and most terrible moments of his life that he was most conscious of this heavenly peace, *e.g.,* during the first night after he had been driven out of his father's home; on a cold night in inhospitable Tibet; in prison at Ilom, Nepal; in the horrible mortuary at Rasar in Tibet, when he was thrown into a well which was full of dead bodies. According to the Sadhu, the physical suffering was great, but in spirit he was happy. He saw then more clearly than ever that Jesus was alive and that it was He who filled his heart with peace and joy. In those moments of joy, hell became heaven.

He also used to say: "When I had to suffer for my Saviour I found heaven on earth; that is a wonderful joy, which I did not feel at other times. In suffering I have always had such a strong sense of the Presence of Christ that no doubt could cross my mind. His presence was radiant as the sun at noonday."

For him suffering was the way to communion with God and to blessedness:

> The cross is like the fruit of the walnut-tree. The outer rind is bitter, but the kernel is refreshing and strengthening. From the outside the cross has neither beauty nor goodness; its essence is only revealed to those who bear it. They find a kernel of spiritual sweetness and inward peace.

> During an earthquake it sometimes happens that *fresh springs* break out in dry places which water and quicken the land so that plants can grow. In the same way, the shattering experiences of suffering can cause the living water to well up in a human heart.

> A newborn child cries, for only in this way will his lungs expand. A doctor once told me of a child who could not breathe when he was born. In order to make him breathe the doctor gave him a slight blow. The mother must have thought the doctor cruel. But he was really doing the

kindest thing possible. As with newborn children the lungs are contracted, so are our spiritual lungs. *But through suffering God strikes us in love.* Then our lungs expand and we can breathe and pray.

Prof. F. Heiler said: "Suffering and the cross are the means which God uses to give to men the deepest and purest blessedness. But the cross does not bring only blessedness to man, it makes him like God. Because the Saviour of the world Himself endured suffering and the cross, in the like manner humanity_becomes transformed into His likeness through the cross and through suffering. True suffering is part of Christian mysticism; it draws the Christian into the closest living fellowship with Christ. It is a great privilege, a great honour to enter into 'the fellowship of His suffering.' Hence it is Sundar Singh's earnest desire in all things to follow the example of the suffering Christ. In all the suspicions and accusations hurled at him by his opponents, he keeps steadily before his eyes the picture of the silent Christ before the Sanhedrin. And as he wished to suffer with Christ, so also he desired to die with Him."

Sundar Singh said, "Because I am glad to share in the sufferings of Christ I have no desire to experience His return while I am yet alive... Rather I long to do as He did, to die, and through the gate of death to enter heaven, that I may *understand* something of what is meant to Him to die for us."

Like other great Christian martyrs and mystics, Sundar Singh is a true *Lover of the Cross*: "The cross is the key to Heaven. There is nothing higher than the cross in earth or heaven. Through the Cross God reveals His love for man. Without the Cross we should know nothing of the love of our Heavenly Father. For this reason God desires all His children to bear this heavy but sweet burden; for only in this way can our love for God and His for us become visible to others. To follow Christ and to carry His cross is so sweet and precious that if I find no cross to bear in heaven I shall beseech Him to send me into hell, if that be possible, in order that at least I may have the opportunity of bearing His Cross. His presence can turn hell into heaven."

However, the supernatural power of the Cross reveals itself only to him who accepts it with humility and gratitude. "If you gladly carry the Cross, He will carry you and lead you to your desired goal." In these words of the *Imitation of Christ*, Sundar Singh again expresses his inmost personal experience.

"Out of my long experience as a sadhu and sanyasi for Christ's sake, I can say with confidence that the Cross will bear those who bear the Cross, until it bears them up to heaven, into the actual presence of the glorified Redeemer." (*The Gospel of Sadhu Sundar Singh* by F. Heiler).

CHAPTER 14

Gospel and Glory of the Cross

According to the scriptures, there is a Divine necessity for the death of Christ. It was neither arbitrary nor accidental. All the writers of the New Testament insist upon its necessity. In the Gospels, our Lord insisted upon its necessity. "As Moses lifted up the serpent in the wilderness, even so must the Son of Man (Jesus) be lifted up" (Jn 3:14-15). After the Confession of Peter at Caesarea Philippi (Mt 16:13-16), His teaching centered on the Cross. "From that time Jesus began to show to His disciples that He *must* go to Jerusalem, and suffer many things from the elders and chief priests and scribes, and be killed, and be raised again the third day(Mt 16:21)." All the later teaching of Jesus centres on that *must*.

Christ died for our sins and for the sins of the world. In all the teaching of the New Testament, Christ is set forth as taking the place of the sinner in His death. Out of too many passages, one or two of the great passages may be quoted. Paul says, "Christ died for the ungodly...He commandeth His own love towards us, in that, while we were yet sinners, Christ died for us" (Rom 5: 6, 8). "He made Him who knew no sin *to be* sin for us, that we might become the righteousness of God in Him" (2 Cor 5:21). "Christ also suffered for you...who His own self bare our sins in His body upon the tree" (1 Pet 2:21-24). "He is the propitiation (atonement) for our sins, and not for ours only, but also for the whole world" (1 Jn 2:2). "Christ suffered the just for the unjust, that He might bring us to God' (1 Pet 3:18). "Who loved me, and gave Himself up for me" (Gal 2:20).

God was in Christ in all the suffering of redemption. The Son was the gift of Father's love. Herein was the love of God manifested in us, that God sent His Son to be the propitiation for our sins. The Cross is the Supreme manifestation of divine love, but it is that because it was for our sins He died. The problem of redemption was to find a way by which God could be just and the Justifier of the ungodly. Through the death of Christ, God is just and the Justifier of them that believe in Jesus.

Behind the sins there is the sin. Sin may be pardoned, but unless the sin can be purged, the root of the evil will remain. Through faith, the blood (of Jesus) cleanses as well as cancels. The gospel of the Cross is that "The Blood of Jesus Christ His Son cleanseth from all sin." The believer is not only crucified with Christ, he is alive in Christ and Christ lives in him. He is dead to sin, dead to self, dead to the world, dead to the law, and he is alive in Christ, identified with Christ, indwelt by Christ. It is Christ that saves. There is no salvation in the Cross, but in the Christ that died and rose again. We are justified by faith (Eph 2:8).

The Cross is the first fact of the gospel of Christ. All the apostles gave it the first place. The Cross is central. Instead of keeping the Cross in the background they set it forth. It became the symbol of new faith. St. Paul made it the central theme of his preaching. He gloried in the Cross. To the Corinthians, he wrote, "I determined to know nothing among you save Jesus Christ and Him crucified" (1 Cor 2:2); and again he summed up the gospel in the words,

"We preach Christ Crucified." To the Galatians, he wrote, "God forbid that I should glory save in the cross of our Lord Jesus Christ." So it was with all the apostles. To John, Jesus is the Lamb of God and the propitiation (atonement) for the sin of the world (Jn 1:29), and Peter attributes the experience of salvation to the precious blood of Christ (1 Pet 1:19-20). Everywhere in the preaching and teaching of the apostles the Cross was the basis of faith, the substance of gospel and the inspiration of holiness and service.

The meaning and interpretation of the death of Christ on the Cross was given by the risen Lord Himself, and He interpreted it according to the scriptures. "And beginning from Moses and from all the prophets, He interpreted to them in all the scriptures the things concerning Himself" (Lk 24:25-27). The wisdom of the world has no key to the meaning of the Cross. No man can say Jesus is Lord save the Holy Ghost, and the Cross is not a theory but a gospel.

The redemption is through the blood of Jesus Christ (1 Pet 1:18-20; Jn 1:29; Rev 12:11; 21:23). The Cross is an incident (i.e., appeared in history in about 30 AD) but the sacrifice is eternal. The lamb slain from the foundation of the world (Rev 13:8; 1 Pet 1:20) is in the midst of the Throne (Phil 2:9; Rev 1:12-18; Acts 2:32-36). The throne is the Throne of Grace. Through the Cross there is preached unto all sinners the gospel of forgiving love. Forgiveness is concerned with more than penalty. The forgiven must forgive. The Cross begets Godliness in those who receive its gospel.

The Cross is a symbol of experience and an object of faith. The believer is conformed to the death of the Cross and is quickened by the power of resurrection. It is not a philosophy, nor a theology, but a fellowship. "I have been crucified with Christ, nevertheless I live, yet not I, but Christ lives in me ; and the life which I now live in flesh, I live by the faith of the Son of God, who loved me, and gave Himself for me" (Gal 2 :20).

Sign of Christian Discipleship

The Cross is the sign by which disciples of Christ are known— because they live by the Cross. It is both a symbol and a memorial. As mentioned earlier, the logic of the Cross is found in Gal 2:20. There has to be a death before there can be a resurrection, but the resurrection ratifies death and brings the power of new life in fellowship with the risen Saviour.

The two eternal principles revealed in the Cross of our Lord are the absolute obedience to the Will of God His Father and the absolute outpouring of Himself for others. Jesus was true and loyal to the will of the Father (Ps 40: 6-8; Heb 10: 5-7). The will of the Father was His meat and drink, and His joy was in all things to do the things that were pleasing to Him (Jn 4:34; 6:38). The second comprehensive principle revealed in the death of Christ is the outpouring of Himself in redeeming love and compassion for others."He gave Himself." He could not save Himself because He came to save others. So no man who spares himself can be His disciple, conformed to His death! "Hereby know we love, because He laid down His life for us; and we ought to lay down our lives for the brethren (1 Jn 3:16).

Chadwick's Views on Discipleship and Suffering

The badge of the disciple is the Cross. Our Lord did not spare its implications of hardship, persecution, alienation and heart break. Those who would follow Him must consider who it was they chose to follow and the path He trod. Those who follow the Man of Sorrows (Isaiah 53) must be prepared to share His grief. The way of the kingdom was by way of the Cross (Mt 7:13-14; 28:18-20). The Cross was the instrument of condemnation, the symbol of reproach, the sign of the curse, and no man could or can be a disciple who does not take up his cross and follow his Lord. The disciple of Christ renounces all *proprietorship* in himself, all ownership of his possessions, all control of his life. He is not his own, and all that he has is at the absolute disposal of Jesus Christ, once a Nazarene carpenter, afterwards a homeless prophet and a condemned and forsaken Leader who was crucified between two criminals. Those who follow Him must tread where he trod, share His lot and make His cause their own; and the New Testament message insists that discipleship involves fellowship of His sufferings. The work of suffering was completed, and on the Cross our Lord declared His sacrifice to be a finished work. The power of His resurrection can be followed by the fellowship of His sufferings. It is true that the bleeding Lamb (Jesus) is eternally in the midst of the Throne, but the Lamb represents a completed redemption and a continuous redeeming ministry. The blood shed for our redemption was shed once for all in the sacrifice of Calvary, but the pouring out of life in the salvation of the world is eternal, perpetual and effectual. To the fellowship of that redeeming passion we may come through the power of His resurrection.

Suffering is Related to Resurrection and Salvation

Paul says, "That I may know Him, and the power of His resurrection and the fellowship of His suffering, being made conformable unto His death" (Phil 3 :10). Peter says, "Christ also suffered for you, leaving you an example, that you should follow His steps" (1 Pet 2:21). And as disciples of Christ we are called to suffer as He suffered, and not as those who acknowledge no allegiance to Him. Suffering tests character, reveals it, develops it ; and although there is no severe test of discipleship than the way we endure, the purpose of His sufferings was not merely to show us how to suffer. He Himself was made perfect by the things He suffered (Heb 5:6-10). It was by the discipline of suffering that He was made perfect in the Ministry of His heavenly priesthood. He is a Priest upon the Throne. He sits, but He pleads. Intercession mediates. The followers (disciples) share His travail. They pray in His Spirit... They bear His burdens. They carry His cross. They fill up that which is unfinished in His sufferings and His work. For this the apostle counted all things loss, refuse, rubbish...For this he died with Christ, that he might know the power of His resurrection and the fellowship of His sufferings, for this fellowship of power and suffering lies on the Pentecost side of Calvary.

The Suffering Lamb Is the Heavenly Lamb
The lamb is in the midst of the elders and the four living creatures, in the midst of the Throne and of the redeemed. The Lamb is eternal (Rev 4:2-11). The Lamb redeems and saves. The Lamb conquers and rules. The Lamb still bleeds. The altar is the Throne. The victim-Priest is King and Lord. He entered the Holy place "through His own blood," and "having made purification of sins, sat down on the right hand of the Majesty on High."

That is the 'Godward' side of the Cross. Jesus of Nazareth was slain by the hand of lawless men. That is one side of the truth, and it is the earthly side. The heavenly side is that He was God's Lamb, 'delivered up by the determinate foreknowledge and counsel of God.' Therefore, the Lamb stands in the midst 'as though it had been slain.' Slain lambs do not stand, but the *Eternal Lamb stands and bleeds*. The blood is the life. In sacrifice the life is poured forth. Sacrifice is the heart of God and of His universe. He gave! Of the

Lamb it is said, 'He emptied Himself.' The bleeding Lamb is eternally at the heart of Sovereignty and the very soul of Redemption. Jesus Christ exalted, but *He is still the Lamb* (1 Pet 1:18-19) *Jesus is the ruling (reigning) Lamb* (Rev 22:3-5); He is the *shepherding Lamb* (Rev 21:22-27); He is the *Conquering Lamb* (Rev 12:11); He is the *Shining Lamb* (Rev 21:22-27; 22:3-5).

Acharya James Dayal's Views on the Glory of the Cross

The glory of the Cross is not only in Jesus' life sacrificed on the Cross, but in His resurrection from the dead on the third day. If He had not risen from the dead, His death would have no relation with His Redeeming act from the beginning of things (आदि-यज्ञ). Actually, Jesus is the sacrificial Lamb slain in the plan of God from the very foundation of the world, *i.e.*, there was a cross in the heart of God before there was one on Calvary (Rev 13:8; Mt 25:34; Eph 1:4; 1 Pet 1:20). Love and Sacrifice are at the heart of God's sovereignty. Besides, God accepted His sacrifice on the Cross as the redeeming act for the whole mankind and put His seal on this great act.

Christ's death on the Cross is an indication of how God's heart was broken (Ps 22; Isa 53) to bring humanity into contact with Him (Jn 3:16). Acharya Dayal gives more insights into the Cross:

(1) The Cross is the *fatwa* (edict) of God's judgment given to all mankind (Lk 7: 29-30).

(2) The Cross is the price paid for the redemption of mankind from the grip or bond of death (Rom 7:18; 1 Cor 7:23; 1 Cor 6:20; Jn 19:30).

(3) The Cross of Christ broke the sting of death and made it powerless (1 Cor 15:55; Jn 18:38; Mt 27:45-46). Then Jesus said, "I am the resurrection and the life" (Jn 11:25).

(4) The Cross is a great spiritual struggle between death and the victorious power of the Prince of peace (Jesus)– this great spiritual struggle ultimately swallowed up death in victory (1 Cor 15:54-55; Isa 25:8).

(5) The Cross is a place where the older self is executed and the devotee is granted a new life through faith (Gal 2:20) There God's mercy and judgment meet together. The Cross is the arm of the Lord extended to save sinners (cf Isa 53:1).

(6) The Cross is the revelation of Christ's love–movement by which He expresses the secret of His unique love which takes believers to heaven or eternal life (Jn 3:16).This means that God allowed His un-manifest Word to become flesh (manifest form) so that He might shed His blood as a price for the redemption of mankind (1 Pet 1 : 18-20).

(7) The Cross is a bridge built by God for true devotees to reach the shore or goal of their life; those who feel the need of this bridge, receive redemption by accepting Christ.

Let the readers know and be convinced that Jesus the Sadguru is the True Teacher, the manifest form of the un-manifest God, eternal and pre-existent (Jn 1:1-2, 14;3:2; 10:30; 14:6, 9-11; Rom 9:5; Col 1:15; 2:9; Heb 1:1-3, etc.). Jesus' disciples used to call Him "Guru" and "Lord" and Jesus affirmed it (Jn 13:13). God's love has given us the Sadguru. This Sadguru is looking for sincere disciples— those who love to followHis commandments (Lk 9: 23-25; Mt 7:21-23; 10:37-38 etc.) and lead a crucified life of self-denial, sacrifice and suffering in order to reach the "goal" or "destination" (2 Cor 5:1; 2 Pet 3:13).